當代中文課程

A Course in Contemporary Chinese

編寫教師・王佩卿、陳慶華、黃桂英
主編・鄧守信

二版

Textbook

課本

1-3

國立臺灣師範大學國語教學中心 策劃
Mandarin Training Center National Taiwan Normal University

序 Foreword

　　臺灣師範大學國語教學中心成立於 1956 年，是臺灣歷史最悠久、規模最完備、教學最有成效的華語文教學機構。每年培育三千名以上的外籍學生，學生來自世界一百二十餘國，至今累計人數已達五萬餘人，在國際間享譽盛名。

　　本中心自 1967 年開始編製教材，迄今共計編寫五十餘本教材，在華語教學界具有舉足輕重之地位。而現今使用之主教材已有十五年之久，不少學生及教師認為現行教材內容需要更新，應新編配合時代需求的新教材。因此，本中心因應外在環境變遷、教學法及教學媒體的創新與進步，籌畫編寫《當代中文課程》6 冊，以符合海內外華語教學的需求，並強化臺灣華語文教學教材之品牌。

　　為了讓理論與實務結合，並落實發揚華語文教學的精神與理念，本中心邀請了華語教學界的大師——鄧守信教授擔任主編，率領 18 位極富教學經驗的第一線老師進行內容編寫，並由張莉萍副研究員、張黛琪老師及教材研發組成員蔡如珮、張雯雯擔任執行編輯，進行了這項《當代中文課程》的編寫計畫。

　　這是本中心歷經數十年深厚教學經驗後再次開發的全新主教材，更為了確保品質，特別慎重；我們很榮幸地邀請到美國的 Claudia Ross 教授、白建華教授及陳雅芬教授，擔任顧問，也邀請了臺灣的葉德明教授、美國的姚道中教授及大陸的劉珣教授，擔任審查委員，並由本校英語系李櫻教授和畢永峨教授分別協助生詞和語法的翻譯。此教材在本中心及臺灣其他語言中心，進行了一年多的試用；經過顧問的悉心指導、審查委員的仔細批閱，並參考了老師及學生提出的寶貴意見，再由編寫老師做了多次修改，才將版本定稿。對於所有在編寫過程中，努力不懈的編輯團隊、給予指教的教授、配合試用的老師及學生，我們都要致上最高的謝意。

　　在此也特別感謝聯經出版事業股份有限公司，願意投注最大的心力，以專業的製作出版能力，協助我們將這套教材以最佳品質問世。

　　我們希望，《當代中文課程》不只提供學生們一套實用有效的教材，亦讓老師得到愉快充實的教學經驗。歡迎老師在使用後，給予我們更多的指教與建議，讓我們不斷進步，也才能為海內外的華語教學，做更多更好的貢獻。

臺灣師範大學國語教學中心主任　陳浩然

The Mandarin Training Center (MTC) at National Taiwan Normal University (NTNU) was established in 1956, and is the oldest, most comprehensive, and most pedagogically effective educational institute of its kind in Taiwan. Every year over 3,000 international students are trained at MTC, and to the present day over 50,000 students representing more than 120 countries have walked through its doors, solidifying international renown.

MTC started producing teaching material in 1967, and has since completed over 50 textbooks, making it a frontrunner in the field of teaching Chinese as a second language. As the core books have been in circulation for 15 years already, many students and teachers agree that updates are in order, and that new materials should be made to meet the modern demand. Changes in the social landscape, improved teaching methods, and innovations in educational media are what prompted the production of MTC's six-volume series, *A Course in Contemporary Chinese*. The project responds to Chinese teaching needs both at home and abroad, and bolsters Taiwan's brand of teaching material for Chinese as a second language.

With the goal of integrating theory and practice, and carrying forward the spirit of teaching Chinese as a second language, MTC petitioned one of the field's most esteemed professors, Shou-Hsin Teng, to serve as chief editor. *A Course in Contemporary Chinese* has been compiled and edited under his leadership, together with the help of 18 seasoned Chinese teachers and the following four executive editors: Associate Research Fellow Liping Chang, Tai-chi Chang, and Ru-pei Cai and Wen-wen Chang of the MTC teaching material development division.

MTC is presenting this brand new core material after half a century's worth of educational experience, and we have taken extra care to ensure it is of uncompromised quality. We were delighted to have American professors Claudia Ross, Jianhua Bai , and Yea-fen Chen act as consultants, Professor Teh-Ming Yeh from Taiwan, Professor Tao-chung Yao from the U.S., and Professor Xun Liu from China on the review committee, and professors Ying Cherry Li and Yung-O Biq of NTNU's English department help with the respective translation of vocabulary and grammar points. The material was first trialed at MTC and other language centers around Taiwan for a year. The current version underwent numerous drafts, and materialized under the careful guidance of the consultants, a sedulous reading from the review committee, and feedback from teachers and students. As for the editorial process, we owe the greatest thanks to the indefatigable editorial team, the professors and their invaluable input, and the teachers and students who were willing to trial the book.

An additional and special thanks is due to Linking Publishing Company, who put forth utmost effort and professionalism in publishing this set of teaching material, allowing us to deliver a publication of superior quality.

It is our hope that *A Course in Contemporary Chinese* is not merely a practical set of teaching materials for students, but also enriching for teachers and the entire teaching experience. We welcome comments from instructors who have put the books into practice so that we can continue improving the material. Only then can we keep furthering our contribution to the field of teaching Chinese as a second language, both in Taiwan and abroad.

Hao Jan Chen
Director of the Mandarin Training Center
National Taiwan Normal University

From the Editor's Desk

Finally, after more than two years, volume one of our six-volume project is seeing the light of day. The language used in *A Course in Contemporary Chinese* is up to date, and though there persists a deep 'generation gap' between it and my own brand of Chinese, this is as it should be. In addition to myself, our project team has consisted of 18 veteran MTC teachers and the entire staff of the MTC Section of Instructional Materials, plus the MTC Deputy Director.

The field of L2 Chinese in Taiwan seems to have adopted the world-famous 'one child policy'. The complete set of currently used textbooks was born a generation ago, and until now has been without predecessor. We are happy to fill this vacancy, and with the title 'number two', yet we also aspire to have it be number two in name alone. After a generation, we present a slightly disciplined contemporary language as observed in Taiwan, we employ Hanyu Pinyin without having to justify it cautiously and timidly, we are proud to present a brand-new system of Chinese parts of speech that will hopefully eliminate many instances of error, we have devised two kinds of exercises in our series, one basically structural and the other entirely task-based, each serving its own intended function, and finally we have included in each lesson a special aspect of Chinese culture. Moreover, all this is done in full color, the first time ever in the field of L2 Chinese in Taiwan. The settings for our current series is in Taipei, Taiwan, with events taking place near the National Taiwan Normal University. The six volumes progress from basic colloquial to semi-formal and finally to authentic conversations or narratives. The glossary in vocabulary and grammar is in basically semi-literal English, not free translation, as we wish to guide the readers/learners along the Chinese 'ways of thinking', but rest assured that no pidgin English has been used.

I am a functional, not structural, linguist, and users of our new textbooks will find our approaches and explanations more down to earth. Both teachers and learners will find that the content resonates with their own experiences and feelings. Rote learning plays but a tiny part of our learning experiences. In a functional frame, the role of the speaker often seen as prominent. This is natural, as numerous adverbs in Chinese, as they are traditionally referred to, do not in fact modify verb phrases at all. They relate to the speaker.

We, the field of Chinese as a second language, know a lot about how to teach, especially when it comes to Chinese characters. Most L2 Chinese teachers world-wide are ethnically Chinese, and teach characters just as they were taught in childhood. Truth is, we know next to nothing how adult students/learners actually learn characters, and other elements of the Chinese language. While we have nothing new in this series of textbooks that contributes to the teaching of Chinese characters, I tried to tightly integrate teaching and learning through our presentation of vocabulary items and grammatical structures. Underneath such methodologies is my personal conviction, and at times both instructors' and learners' patience is requested. I welcome communication with all users of our new textbooks, whether instructors or students/learners.

Shou-hsin Teng

Series Introduction

This six-volume series is a comprehensive learning material that focuses on spoken language in the first three volumes and written language in the latter three volumes. Volume One aims to strengthen daily conversation and applications; Volume Two contains short essays as supplementary readings; Volume Three introduces beginning-level written language and discourse, in addition to extended dialogues. Volume Four uses discourse to solidify the learner's written language and ability in reading authentic materials; Volumes Five and Six are arranged in topics such as society, technology, economics, politics, culture, and environment to help the learner expand their language utilizations in different domains.

Each volume includes a textbook, a student workbook, and a teacher's manual. In addition, Volume One and Two include a practice book for characters.

Level of Students

A Course in Contemporary Chinese 《當代中文課程》 is suitable for learners of Chinese in Taiwan, as well as for high school or college level Chinese language courses overseas. Volumes One to Six cover levels A1 to C1 in the CEFR, or Novice to Superior levels in ACTFL Guidelines.

Overview

- The series adopts communicative language teaching and task-based learning to boost the learner's Chinese ability.
- Each lesson has learning objectives and self-evaluation to give the learner a clear record of tasks completed.
- Lessons are authentic daily situations to help the learner learn in natural contexts.
- Lexical items and syntactic structures are presented and explained in functional, not structural, perspectives.
- Syntactic, i.e. grammatical, explanation includes functions, structures, pragmatics, and drills to guide the learner to proper usage.
- Classroom activities have specific learning objectives, activities, or tasks to help fortify learning while having fun.
- The "Bits of Chinese Culture" section of the lesson has authentic photographs to give the learner a deeper look at local Taiwanese culture.
- Online access provides supplementary materials for teachers & students.

改版緣起　Reasons for the Revision

　　《當代中文課程》第一冊出版迄今已六年，在中華文化中，「六」這個數字象徵著吉祥，也代表了和諧融洽的意涵。我們將六年以來所接獲的各方意見，彙整之後進行教材改版，希望能藉由教材的新面貌，答謝讀者這些日子以來對《當代中文課程》的支持與愛護。

　　新版《當代中文課程》在紙本教材方面，不僅修訂教材內容，也調整了分冊形式，便於讀者攜帶；在數位方面則改善了音檔下載的使用流程，讓操作更加流暢。此外，我們為每課對話製作擴增實境（Augmented Reality，簡稱 AR）動畫，增添教材的數位互動性。讀者只需將行動裝置（手機或平板）掃描課本中的課文插圖，就能看到生動的動畫。文字搭配動態圖像使學習更富樂趣，並有助於強化記憶，自然而然地提升學習成效。

　　《當代中文課程》編著團隊致力於落實「當代」之名，讓此套教材在任何時刻都順應潮流，符合當代語彙，符合當代中文學習者的使用需求。以此考量，推出新版《當代中文課程》，若未來讀者有任何新期許，也歡迎繼續賜教。

　　It has been six years since the first volume of *A Course in Contemporary Chinese* was published. For Chinese culture, the number "six" symbolizes good luck and also means harmony and rapport. We have further consolidated the diverse opinions we have received over the past six years and then revised the teaching materials. With the new look of textbooks, we are eager to thank readers for their support and love to *A Course in Contemporary Chinese* over the past few years.

　　In terms of paper textbooks, the new edition of *A Course in Contemporary Chinese* has not only revised the content of the textbooks, but also adjusted the format to several volumes to make it easy for readers to carry. Regarding the digital aspect, the use process of audio file download has been optimized to make the operation smoother. On top of that, we create augmented reality (AR for short) animations for the dialogues of each lesson, which adds to the digital interactivity of the teaching materials. Therefore, readers only need to scan the text illustrations in the textbook with their mobile devices (mobile phones or tablets) to see vivid animations. Based on this, this textbook is composed of text and dynamic images to make learning more fun, and helps strengthen readers' memory and promote learning effectiveness.

　　The editorial team of *A Course in Contemporary Chinese* is dedicated to implementing the name "Contemporary," hoping to make this set of textbooks follow the trend of the generation at all times and meet the needs of contemporary vocabulary and contemporary Chinese learners. In view of this, we launched a new version of *A Course in Contemporary Chinese*. If future readers have any new related expectations, please continue to remind us.

1. 使用行動裝置（手機或平板）免費下載 MAKAR APP （僅限 iOS 及 Android 系統）

   Readers are invited to use mobile devices (mobile phones or tablets) to download MAKAR APP for free (iOS and Android systems only).

App Store (iOS)　　　Google Play (Android)

2. 開啟 MAKAR APP

   Enable MAKAR APP

① 點擊「搜尋」　　　　　　　　　　　　Click "Search"

② 於搜尋欄位中輸入「Dangdai」　　　　Enter "Dangdai" in the search field

③ 點擊「專案」　　　　　　　　　　　　Click "Project"

④ 點擇任一專案（無須對照課數）　　　　Click any project (no need to match the number of courses)

⑤ 點擊「開始體驗」　　　　　　　　　　Click "Start Experience"

⑥ 掃描《當代中文課程》課本的課文插圖即可播放動畫

   Scan the illustrations of the text in the textbook of *A Course in Contemporary Chinese* to start playing the animation.

An Introduction to the Chinese Language

China is a multi-ethnic society, and when people in general study Chinese, 'Chinese' usually refers to the Beijing variety of the language as spoken by the Han people in China, also known as Mandarin Chinese or simply Mandarin. It is the official language of China, known mostly domestically as the Putonghua, the lingua franca, or Hanyu, the Han language. In Taiwan, Guoyu refers to the national/official language, and Huayu to either Mandarin Chinese as spoken by Chinese descendants residing overseas, or to Mandarin when taught to non-Chinese learners. The following pages present an outline of the features and properties of Chinese. For further details, readers are advised to consult various and rich on-line resources.

Language Kinship

Languages in the world are grouped together on the basis of language affiliation, called language-family. Chinese, or rather Hanyu, is a member of the Sino-Tibetan family, which covers most of China today, plus parts of Southeast Asia. Therefore, Tibetan, Burmese, and Thai are genetically related to Hanyu.

Hanyu is spoken in about 75% of the present Chinese territory, by about 75% of the total Chinese population, and it covers 7 major dialects, including the better known Cantonese, Hokkienese, Hakka and Shanghainese.

Historically, Chinese has interacted highly actively with neighboring but unaffiliated languages, such as Japanese, Korean and Vietnamese. The interactions took place in such areas as vocabulary items, phonological structures, a few grammatical features and most importantly the writing script.

Typological Features of Chinese

Languages in the world are also grouped together on the basis of language characteristics, called language typology. Chinese has the following typological traits, which highlight the dissimilarities between Chinese and English.

A. Chinese is a non-tense language. Tense is a grammatical device such that the verb changes according to the time of the event in relation to the time of utterance. Thus 'He talks nonsense' refers to his habit, while 'He talked nonsense' refers to a time in the past when he behaved that way, but he does not necessarily do that all the time. 'Talked' then is a verb in the past tense. Chinese does not operate with this device but marks the time of events with time expressions such as 'today' or 'tomorrow' in the sentence. The verb remains the same regardless of time of happening. This type of language is labeled as an atensal language, while English and most European languages are tensal languages. Knowing this particular trait can help European learners of Chinese avoid mistakes to do with verbs in Chinese. Thus, in responding to 'What did you do in China last year?' Chinese is 'I teach English (last year)'; and to 'What are you doing now in Japan?' Chinese is again 'I teach English (now)'.

B. Nouns in Chinese are not directly countable. Nouns in English are either countable, e.g. 2 candies, or non-countable, e.g. *2 salts, while all nouns in Chinese are non-countable. When they are to be counted, a measure, or called classifier, must be used between a noun and a number, e.g. 2-piece-candy. Thus, Chinese is a classifier language. Only non-countable nouns in English are used with measures, e.g. a drop of water.

Therefore it is imperative to learn nouns in Chinese together with their associated measures/classifiers. There are only about 30 high-frequency measures/classifiers in Chinese to be mastered at the initial stage of learning.

C. Chinese is a Topic-Prominent language. Sentences in Chinese quite often begin with somebody or something that is being talked about, rather than the subject of the verb in the sentence. This item is called a topic in linguistics. Most Asian languages employ topic, while most European languages employ subject. The following bad English sentences, sequenced below per frequency of usage, illustrate the topic structures in Chinese.

*Senator Kennedy, people in Europe also respected.

*Seafood, Taiwanese people love lobsters best.

*President Obama, he attended Harvard University.

Because of this feature, Chinese people tend to speak 'broken' English, whereas English speakers tend to sound 'complete', if bland and alien, when they talk in Chinese. Through practice and through keen observations of what motivates the use of a topic in Chinese, this feature of Chinese can be acquired eventually.

D. Chinese tends to drop things in the sentence. The 'broken' tendencies mentioned above also include not using nouns in a sentence where English counterparts are 'complete'. This tendency is called dropping, as illustrated below through bad English sentences.

Are you coming tomorrow? ----- *Come!

What did you buy? ----- *Buy some jeans.

*This bicycle, who rides? ----- *My old professor rides.

The 1st example drops everything except the verb, the 2nd drops the subject, and the 3rd drops the object. Dropping happens when what is dropped is easily recoverable or identifiable from the contexts or circumstances. Not doing this, Europeans are often commented upon that their sentences in Chinese are too often inundated with unwanted pronouns!!

Phonological Characteristics of Chinese

Phonology refers to the system of sound, the pronunciation, of a language. To untrained ears, Chinese language sounds unfamiliar, sort of alien in a way. This is due to the fact that Chinese sound system contains some elements that are not part of the sound systems of European languages, though commonly found on the Asian continent. These features will be explained below.

On the whole, the Chinese sound system is not really very complicated. It has 7 vowels, 5 of which are found in English (i, e, a, o, u), plus 2 which are not (-e,); and it has 21 consonants, 15 of which are quite common, plus 6 which are less common (zh, ch, sh, r, z, c). And Chinese has a fairly simple syllable shape, i.e. consonant + vowel plus possible nasals (n or ng). What is most striking to English speakers is that every syllable in Chinese has a 'tone', as will be detailed directly below. But, a word on the sound representation, the pinyin system, first.

A. Hanyu Pinyin. Hanyu Pinyin is a variety of Romanization systems that attempt to represent the sound of Chinese through the use of Roman letters (abc...). Since the end of the 19th century, there have been about half a dozen Chinese Romanization systems, including the Wade-Giles, Guoyu Luomazi, Yale, Hanyu Pinyin, Lin Yutang, and Zhuyin Fuhao Di'ershi, not to mention the German system, the French system etc. Thanks to the consensus of media worldwide, and through the support of the UN, Hanyu Pinyin has become the standard worldwide. Taiwan is probably the only place in the world that does not support nor employ Hanyu Pinyin. Instead, it uses non-Roman symbols to represent the sound, called Zhuyin Fuhao, alias BoPoMoFo (cf. the symbols employed in this volume). Officially, that is. Hanyu Pinyin represents the Chinese sound as follows.

b, p, m, f　d, t, n, l　g, k, h　j, q, x　zh, ch, sh, r　z, c, s

a, o, -e, e　ai, ei, ao, ou　an, en, ang, eng　-r, i, u, ü

B. Chinese is a tonal language. A tone refers to the voice pitch contour. Pitch contours are used in many languages, including English, but for different functions in different languages. English uses them to indicate the speaker's viewpoints, e.g. 'well' in different contours may indicate impatience, surprise, doubt etc. Chinese, on the other hand, uses contours to refer to different meanings, words. Pitch contours with different linguistic functions are not transferable from one language to another. Therefore, it would be futile trying to learn Chinese tones by looking for or identifying their contour counterparts in English.

Mandarin Chinese has 4 distinct tones, the fewest among all Han dialects, i.e. level, rising, dipping and falling, marked ‾ ⁄ ∨ ＼, and it has only one tone-change rule, i.e. ∨ ∨ → ⁄ ∨, though the conditions for this change are fairly complicated. In addition to the four tones, Mandarin also has one neutral(ized) tone, i.e.·, pronounced short/unstressed, which is derived, historically if not synchronically, from the 4 tones; hence the term neutralized. Again, the conditions and environments for the neutralization are highly complex and cannot be explored in this space.

C. Syllable final −r effect (vowel retroflexivisation). The northern variety of Hanyu, esp. in Beijing, is known for its richness in the −r effect at the end of a syllable. For example, 'flower' is 'huā' in southern China but 'huār' in Beijing. Given the prominence of the city Beijing, this sound feature tends to be defined as standard nationwide; but that −r effect is rarely attempted in the south. There do not seem to be rigorous rules governing what can and what cannot take the −r effect. It is thus advised that learners of Chinese resort to rote learning in this case, as probably even native speakers of northern Chinese do.

D. Syllables in Chinese do not 'connect'. 'Connect' here refers to the merging of the tail of a syllable with the head of a subsequent syllable, e.g. English pronounces 'at' + 'all' as 'at+tall', 'did' +'you' as 'did+dyou' and 'that'+'is' as 'that+th'is'. On the other hand, syllables in Chinese are isolated from each other and do not connect in this way. Fortunately, this is not a serious problem for English language learners, as the syllable structures in Chinese are rather limited, and there are not many candidates for this merging. We noted above that Chinese syllables take the form of CV plus possible 'n' and 'ng'. CV does not give rise to connecting, not even in English; so be extra cautious when a syllable ends with 'n' or 'g' and a subsequent syllable begins with a V, e.g. MǐnÀo 'Fujian Province and Macao'. Nobody would understand 'min+nao'!!

E. Retroflexive consonants. 'Retroflexive' refers to consonants that are pronounced with the tip of the tongue curled up (-flexive) backwards (retro-). There are altogether 4 such consonants, i.e. zh, ch, sh, and r. The pronunciation of these consonants reveals the geographical origin of native Chinese speakers. Southerners do not have them, merging them with z, c, and s, as is commonly observed in Taiwan. Curling up of the tongue comes in various degrees. Local Beijing dialect is well known for its prominent curling. Imagine curling up the tongue at the beginning of a syllable and curling it up again for the –r effect!! ! Try 'zhèr-over here', 'zhuōr-table' and 'shuǐr-water'.

On Chinese Grammar

'Grammar' refers to the ways and rules of how words are organized into a string that is a sentence in a language. Given the fact that all languages have sentences, and at the same time non-sentences, all languages including Chinese have grammar. In this section, the most salient and important features and issues of Chinese grammar will be presented, but a summary of basic structures, as referenced against English, is given first.

A. Similarities in Chinese and English.

	English	Chinese
SVO	They sell coffee.	Tāmen mài kāfēi.
AuxV+Verb	You may sit down!	Nǐ kěyǐ zuòxià ō!
Adj+Noun	sour grapes	suān pútáo
Prep+its Noun	at home	zài jiā
Num+Meas+Noun	a piece of cake	yí kuài dàngāo
Demons+Noun	those students	nàxiē xuéshēng

B. Dissimilar structures.

	English	Chinese
RelClause: Noun	the book that you bought	nǐ mǎi de shū
VPhrase: PrepPhrase	to eat at home	zài jiā chīfàn
Verb: Adverbial	Eat slowly!	Mànmār chī!

Set: Subset	6th Sept, 1967	1967 nián 9 yuè 6 hào
	Taipei, Taiwan	Táiwān Táiběi
	3 of my friends…	wǒ de péngyǒu, yǒu sān ge…

C. Modifier precedes modified (MPM). This is one of the most important grammatical principles in Chinese. We see it operating actively in the charts given above, so that adjectives come before nouns they modify, relative clauses also come before the nouns they modify, possessives come before nouns (tā de diànnǎo 'his computer'), auxiliary verbs come before verbs, adverbial phrases before verbs, prepositional phrases come before verbs etc. This principle operates almost without exceptions in Chinese, while in English modifiers sometimes precede and some other times follow the modified.

D. Principle of Temporal Sequence (PTS). Components of a sentence in Chinese are lined up in accordance with the sequence of time. This principle operates especially when there is a series of verbs contained within a sentence, or when there is a sentential conjunction. First compare the sequence of 'units' of an event in English and that in its Chinese counterpart.

Event: David /went to New York/ by train /from Boston/ to see his sister.

English: 1	2	3	4	5
Chinese: 1	4	2	3	5

Now in real life, David got on a train, the train departed from Boston, it arrived in New York, and finally he visited his sister. This sequence of units is 'natural' time, and the Chinese sentence 'Dàwèi zuò huǒchē cóng Bōshìdùn dào Niǔyuē qù kàn tā de jiějie' follows it, but not English. In other words, Chinese complies strictly with PTS.

When sentences are conjoined, English has various possibilities in organizing the conjunction. First, the scenario. H1N1 hits China badly (event-1), and as a result, many schools were closed (event-2). Now, English has the following possible ways of conjoining to express this, e.g.

Many schools were closed, because/since H1N1 hit China badly. (E2+E1)

H1N1 hit China badly, so many schools were closed. (E1+E2)

As H1N1 hit China badly, many schools were closed. (E1+E2)

Whereas the only way of expressing the same in Chinese is E1+E2 when both conjunctions are used (yīnwèi…suǒyǐ…), i.e.

Zhōngguó yīnwèi H1N1 gǎnrǎn yánzhòng (E1), suǒyǐ xǔduō xuéxiào zhànshí guānbì (E2).

PTS then helps explain why 'cause' is always placed before 'consequence' in Chinese.

PTS is also seen operating in the so-called verb-complement constructions in Chinese, e.g. shā-sǐ 'kill+dead', chī-bǎo 'eat+full', dǎ-kū 'hit+cry' etc. The verb represents an action that must have happened first before its consequence.

There is an interesting group of adjectives in Chinese, namely 'zǎo-early', 'wǎn-late', 'kuài-fast', 'màn-slow', 'duō-plenty', and 'shǎo-few', which can be placed either before (as adverbials) or after (as complements) of their associated verbs, e.g.

Nǐ míngtiān zǎo diǎr lái! (Come earlier tomorrow!)

Wǒ lái zǎo le. Jìnbúqù. (I arrived too early. I could not get in.)

When 'zǎo' is placed before the verb 'lái', the time of arrival is intended, planned, but when it is placed after, the time of arrival is not pre-planned, maybe accidental. The difference complies with PTS. The same difference holds in the case of the other adjectives in the group, e.g.

Qǐng nǐ duō mǎi liǎngge! (Please get two extra!)

Wǒ mǎiduō le. Zāotà le! (I bought two too many. Going to be wasted!)

'Duō' in the first sentence is going to be pre-planned, a pre-event state, while in the second, it's a post-event report. Pre-event and post-event states then are naturally taken care of by PTS. Our last set in the group is more complicated. 'Kuài' and 'màn' can refer to amount of time in addition to manner of action, as illustrated below.

Nǐ kuài diǎr zǒu; yào chídào le! (Hurry up and go! You'll be late (e.g. for work)!)

Qǐng nǐ zǒu kuài yìdiǎr! (Please walk faster!)

'Kuài' in the first can be glossed as 'quick, hurry up' (in as little time as possible after the utterance), while that in the second refers to manner of walking. Similarly, 'màn yìdiǎr zǒu-don't leave yet' and 'zǒu màn yìdiǎr-walk more slowly'.

We have seen in this section the very important role in Chinese grammar played by variations in word-order. European languages exhibit rich resources in changing the forms of verbs, adjectives and nouns, and Chinese, like other Asian languages, takes great advantage of word-order.

E. Where to find subjects in existential sentences. Existential sentences refer to sentences in which the verbs express appearing (e.g. coming), disappearing (e.g. going) and presence (e.g. written (on the wall)). The existential verbs are all intransitive, and thus they are all associated with a subject, without any objects naturally. This type of sentences deserves a mention in this introduction, as they exhibit a unique structure in Chinese. When their subjects are in definite reference (something that can be referred to, e.g. pronouns and nouns with definite article in English) the subject appears at the front of the sentence, i.e. before the existential verb, but when their subjects are in indefinite reference (nothing in particular), the subject appears after the verb. Compare the following pair of sentences in Chinese against their counterparts in English.

Kèrén dōu lái le. Chīfàn ba! (All the guests we invited have arrived. Let's serve the dinner.)

Duìbùqǐ! Láiwǎn le. Jiālǐ láile yí ge kèrén. (Sorry for being late! I had an (unexpected) guest.)

More examples of post-verbal subjects are given below.

Zhè cì táifēng sǐle bù shǎo rén. (Quite a few people died during the typhoon this time.)

Zuótiān wǎnshàng xiàle duō jiǔ de yǔ? (How long did it rain last night?)

Zuótiān wǎnshàng pǎole jǐ ge fànrén? (How many inmates got away last night?)

Chēzi lǐ zuòle duōshǎo rén a? (How many people were in the car?)

Exactly when to place the existential subject after the verb will remain a challenge for learners of Chinese for quite a significant period of time. Again, observe and deduce!! Memorising sentence by sentence would not help!!

The existential subjects presented above are simple enough, e.g. people, a guest, rain and inmates. But when the subject is complex, further complications emerge!! A portion of the complex subject stays in front of the verb, and the remaining goes to the back of the verb, e.g.

Míngtiān nǐmen qù jǐge rén? (How many of you will be going tomorrow?)

Wǒ zuìjìn diàole bù shǎo tóufǎ. (I lost=fell quite a lot of hair recently.)

Qùnián dìzhèn, tā sǐle sān ge gēge. (He lost=died 3 brothers during the earthquake last year.)

In linguistics, we say that existential sentences in Chinese have a lot of semantic and information structures involved.

F. A tripartite system of verb classifications in Chinese. English has a clear division between verbs and adjectives, but the boundary in Chinese is quite blurred, which quite seriously misleads English-speaking learners of Chinese. The error in *Wǒ jīntiān shì máng. 'I am busy today.' is a daily observation in Chinese 101! Why is it a common mistake for beginning learners? What do our textbooks and/or teachers do about it, so that the error is discouraged, if not suppressed? Nothing, much! What has not been realized in our profession is that Chinese verb classification is more strongly semantic, rather than more strongly syntactic as in English.

Verbs in Chinese have 3 sub-classes, namely Action Verbs, State Verbs and Process Verbs. Action Verbs are time-sensitive activities (beginning and ending, frozen with a snap-shot, prolonged), are will-controlled (consent or refuse), and usually take human subjects, e.g. 'chī-eat', 'mǎi-buy' and 'xué-learn'. State Verbs are non-time-sensitive physical or mental states, inclusive of the all-famous adjectives as a further sub-class, e.g. 'ài-love', 'xīwàng-hope' and 'liàng-bright'. Process Verbs refer to instantaneous change from one state to another, 'sǐ-die', 'pò-break, burst' and 'wán-finish'.

The new system of parts of speech in Chinese as adopted in this series is built on this very foundation of this tripartite verb classification. Knowing this new system will be immensely helpful in learning quite a few syntactic structures in Chinese that are nicely related to the 3 classes of verbs, as will be illustrated with negation in Chinese in the section below.

The table below presents some of the most important properties of these 3 classes of verbs, as reflected through syntactic behaviour.

	Action Verbs	State Verbs	Process Verbs
Hěn- modification	✗	✓	✗
Le- completive	✓	✗	✓
Zài- progressive	✓	✗	✗
Reduplication	✓ (tentative)	✓ (intensification)	✗
Bù- negation	✓	✓	✗
Méi- negation	✓	✗	✓

Here are more examples of 3 classes of verbs.

Action Verbs: mǎi 'buy', zuò 'sit', xué 'learn; imitate', kàn 'look'

State Verbs: xǐhuān 'like', zhīdào 'know', néng 'can', guì 'expensive'

Process Verbs: wàngle 'forget', chén 'sink', bìyè 'graduate', xǐng 'wake up'

G. Negation. Negation in Chinese is by means of placing a negative adverb immediately in front of a verb. (Remember that adjectives in Chinese are a type of State verbs!) When an action verb is negated with 'bu', the meaning can be either 'intend not to, refuse to' or 'not in a habit of', e.g.

Nǐ bù mǎi piào; wǒ jiù bú ràng nǐ jìnqù! (If you don't buy a ticket, I won't let you in!)

Tā zuótiān zhěng tiān bù jiē diànhuà. (He did not want to answer the phone all day yesterday.)

Dèng lǎoshī bù hē jiǔ. (Mr. Teng does not drink.)

'Bù' has the meaning above but is independent of temporal reference. The first sentence above refers to the present moment or a minute later after the utterance, and the second to the past. A habit again is panchronic. But when an action verb is negated with 'méi(yǒu)', its time reference must be in the past, meaning 'something did not come to pass', e.g.

Tā méi lái shàngbān. (He did not come to work.)

Tā méi dài qián lái. (He did not bring any money.)

A state verb can only be negated with 'bù', referring to the non-existence of that state, whether in the past, at present, or in the future, e.g.

Tā bù zhīdào zhèjiàn shì. (He did not/does not know this.)

Tā bù xiǎng gēn nǐ qù. (He did not/does not want to go with you.)

Niǔyuē zuìjìn bú rè. (New York was/is/will not be hot.)

A process verb can only be negated with 'méi', referring to the non-happening of a change from one state to another, usually in the past, e.g.

Yīfú méi pò; nǐ jiù rēng le? (You threw away perfectly good clothes?)

Niǎo hái méi sǐ; nǐ jiù fàng le ba! (The bird is still alive. Why don't you let it free?)

Tā méi bìyè yǐqián, hái děi dǎgōng. (He has to work odd jobs before graduating.)

As can be gathered from the above, negation of verbs in Chinese follows neat patterns, but this is so only after we work with the new system of verb classifications as presented in this series. Here's one more interesting fact about negation in Chinese before closing this section. When some action verbs refer to some activities that result in something stable, e.g. when you put on clothes, you want the clothes to stay on you, the negation of those verbs can be usually translated in the present tense in English, e.g.

Tā zěnme méi chuān yīfú? (How come he is naked?)

Wǒ jīntiān méi dài qián. (I have no money with me today.)

H. A new system of Parts of Speech in Chinese. In the system of parts of speech adopted in this series, there are at the highest level a total of 8 parts of speech, as given below. This system includes the following major properties. First and foremost, it is errors-driven and can address some of the most prevailing errors exhibited by learners of Chinese. This characteristic dictates the depth of sub-categories in a system of grammatical categories. Secondly, it employs the concept of 'default'. This property greatly simplifies the over-all framework of the new system, so that it reduces the number of categories used, simplifies the labeling of categories, and takes advantage of the learners' contribution in terms of positive transfer. And lastly, it incorporates both semantic as well as syntactic concepts, so that it bypasses the traditionally problematic category of adjectives by establishing three major semantic types of verbs, viz. action, state and process.

Adv	Adverb (dōu 'all', dàgài 'probably')
Conj	Conjunction (gēn 'and', kěshì 'but')
Det	Determiner (zhè 'this', nà 'that')
M	Measure (ge, tiáo; xià, cì)
N	Noun (wǒ 'I', yǒngqì 'courage')
Ptc	Particle (ma 'question particle', le 'completive verbal particle')
Prep	Preposition (cóng 'from', duìyú 'regarding')
V	Action Verb, transitive (mǎi 'buy', chī 'eat')
Vi	Action Verb, intransitive (kū 'cry', zuò 'sit')
Vaux	Auxiliary Verb (néng 'can', xiǎng 'would like to')
V-sep	Separable Verb (jiéhūn 'get married', shēngqì 'get angry')
Vs	State Verb, intransitive (hǎo 'good', guì 'expensive')
Vst	State Verb, transitive (xǐhuān 'like', zhīdào 'know')
Vs-attr	State Verb, attributive (zhǔyào 'primary', xiùzhēn 'mini-')
Vs-pred	State Verb, predicative (gòu 'enough', duō 'plenty')
Vp	Process Verb, intransitive (sǐ 'die', wán 'finish')
Vpt	Process Verb, transitive (pò (dòng) 'lit. break (hole) , liè (fèng) 'lit. crack (a crack))

Notes:

Default values: When no marking appears under a category, a default reading takes place, which has been built into the system by observing the commonest patterns of the highest frequency. A default value can be loosely understood as the most likely candidate. A default system results in using fewer symbols, which makes it easy on the eyes, reducing the amount of processing. Our default readings are as follows.

Default transitivity. When a verb is not marked, i.e. V, it's an action verb. An unmarked action verb, furthermore, is transitive. A state verb is marked as Vs, but if it's not further marked, it's intransitive. The same holds for process verbs, i.e. Vp is by default intransitive.

Default position of adjectives. Typical adjectives occur as predicates, e.g. 'This is great!' Therefore, unmarked Vs are predicative, and adjectives that cannot be predicates will be marked for this feature, e.g. zhǔyào 'primary' is an adjective but it cannot be a predicate, i.e. *Zhètiáo lù hěn zhǔyào. '*This road is very primary.' Therefore it is marked Vs-attr, meaning it can only be used attributively, i.e. zhǔyào dàolù 'primary road'. On the other hand, 'gòu' 'enough' in Chinese can only be used predicatively, not attributively, e.g. 'Shíjiān gòu' '*?Time is enough.', but not *gòu shíjiān 'enough time'. Therefore gòu is marked Vs-pred. Employing this new system of parts of speech guarantees good grammar!

Default wordhood. In English, words cannot be torn apart and be used separately, e.g. *mis- not – understand. Likewise in Chinese, e.g. *xǐbùhuān 'do not like'. However, there is a large group of words in Chinese that are exceptions to this probably universal rule and can be separated. They are called 'separable words', marked -sep in our new system of parts of speech. For example, shēngqì 'angry' is a word, but it is fine to say *shēng tā qì* 'angry at him'. Jiéhūn 'get married' is a word but it's fine to say *jiéguòhūn* 'been married before' or *jié*guò sān cì *hūn* 'been married 3 times before'. There are at least a couple of hundred separable words in modern Chinese. Even native speakers have to learn that certain words can be separated. Thus, memorizing them is the only way to deal with them by learners, and our new system of parts of speech helps them along nicely. Go over the vocabulary lists in this series and look for the marking –sep.

Now, what motivates this severing of words? Ask Chinese gods, not your teachers! We only know a little about the syntactic circumstances under which they get separated. First and foremost, separable words are in most cases intransitive verbs, whether action, state or process. When these verbs are further associated with targets (nouns, conceptual objects), frequency (number of times), duration (for how long), occurrence (done, done away with) etc., separation takes pace and these associated elements are inserted in between. More examples are given below.

Wǒ jīnnián yǐjīng *kǎo*guò 20 cì *shì* le!! (I've taken 20 exams to date this year!)

Wǒ *dào*guò *qiàn* le; tā hái shēngqì! (I apologized, but he's still mad!)

Fàng sān tiān *jià*; dàjiā dōu zǒu le. (There will be a break of 3 days, and everyone has left.)

Final Words

This is a very brief introduction to the modern Mandarin Chinese language, which is the standard world-wide. This introduction can only highlight the most salient properties of the language. Many other features of the language have been left out by design. For instance, nothing has been said about the patterns of word-formations in Chinese, and no presentation has been made of the unique written script of the language. Readers are advised to search on-line for resources relating to particular aspects of the language. For reading, please consult a highly readable best-seller in this regard, viz. Li, Charles and Sandra Thompson. 1982. Mandarin Chinese: a reference grammar. UC Los Angeles Press. (Authorised reprinting by Crane publishing Company, Taipei, Taiwan, still available as of October 2009).

各課重點　**Highlights of Lessons**

Lessons	Topic & Themes	Learning Objectives	Grammar
⓫ I Would Like to Rent a Place	Renting a Place	1. Learning to talk about renting a place to live. 2. Learning to talk about environment of a room or a house. 3. Learning to make requests, e.g., to one's landlord.	1. To Come to Do Something with 來 lái 2. Sooner Than Expected with 就 jiù 3. Existential Subject with 有 yǒu 4. Different Types of 會 huì 5. Omitting Nouns at 2nd Mention
⓬ How Long Do You Plan to Study Chinese in Taiwan?	Study, Work	1. Learning to discuss study plans and future plans. 2. Learning to talk about sequences of events. 3. Learning to describe past actions and experience.	1. 先 xiān…再 zài… *first..., and then ...* 2. To Focus with 是 shì…的 de 3. 以後 yǐhòu *after...* 4. Special Meanings of 好 hǎo / 難 nán + Verbs
⓭ Happy Birthday	Social Life	1. Learning to make appointments on the phone. 2. Learning to ask friends about their dietary preferences. 3. Learning to compare cultures. 4. Learning to express wishes to others on special occasions and to respond appropriately when others offer you wishes on special occasions.	1. 一 yī…就 jiù… *...as soon as...* 2. Completed Action with Verbal 了 le 3. 不 Negation vs. 沒 Negation 4. All-inclusive with Question Words 5. More / less…Than Planned with 多 duō / 少 shǎo + Verb… 6. 是不是 shì bú shì *is it true?* 7. Comparison with 跟 gēn…一樣 yíyàng
⓮ It's So Cold!	The Weather	1. Learning to talk about weather conditions, including typhoons. 2. Learning to talk about the four seasons and explain why you like or dislike them. 3. Learning to compare events. 4. Learning to make simple statements about experiences, e.g., trips.	1. Time-Duration after Verbal 了 le 2. Completion-to-date with Double 了 le 3. 快 kuài…了 le *about to* 4. Comparison 更 gèng *even more so* 5. Inferior Comparison 沒有 méi yǒu…
⓯ I Don't Feel Well	Falling Sick	1. Learning to ask someone how they are feeling. 2. Learning to describe symptoms in simple terms. 3. Learning to give suggestions to somebody who is sick. 4. Learning to reject or accept suggestions.	1. Non-committal Stance with Question Words 2. To Dispose of Something with 把 bǎ 3. V 了 le…就 jiù… *do...right after doing...* 4. 一點 yìdiǎn *a bit* 5. Comparing Actions with a 得 de Complement 6. Complements of Degree in Comparison Structures 7. Separable Verbs

Bits of Chinese Culture	Notes on Pinyin and Pronunciation	Introduction to Chinese Characters
Renting a Place in Taiwan		
1. Addressing People in the Workplace 2. Privacy Means Something Different for Taiwanese		
1. Congratulatory Expressions in Chinese 2. Taiwanese Birthdays		
Typhoon Days-Off		
Wearing Surgical Masks		

Parts of Speech in Chinese

List of Parts of Speech in Chinese

Symbols	Parts of speech	八大詞類	Examples
N	noun	名詞	水、五、昨天、學校、他、幾
V	verb	動詞	吃、告訴、容易、快樂、知道、破
Adv	adverb	副詞	很、不、常、到處、也、就、難道
Conj	conjunction	連詞	和、跟、而且、雖然、因為
Prep	preposition	介詞	從、對、向、跟、在、給
M	measure	量詞	個、張、碗、次、頓、公尺
Ptc	particle	助詞	的、得、啊、嗎、完、掉、把、喂
Det	determiner	限定詞	這、那、某、每、哪

Verb Classification

Symbols	Classification	動詞分類	Examples
V	transitive action verbs	及物動作動詞	買、做、說
Vi	intransitive action verbs	不及物動作動詞	跑、坐、睡、笑
V-sep	intransitive action verbs, separable	不及物動作離合詞	唱歌、上網、打架
Vs	intransitive state verbs	不及物狀態動詞	冷、高、漂亮
Vst	transitive state verbs	及物狀態動詞	關心、喜歡、同意
Vs-attr	intransitive state verbs, attributive only	唯定不及物狀態動詞	野生、公共、新興
Vs-pred	intransitive state verbs, predicative only	唯謂不及物狀態動詞	夠、多、少
Vs-sep	intransitive state verbs, separable	不及物狀態離合詞	放心、幽默、生氣
Vaux	auxiliary verbs	助動詞	會、能、可以
Vp	intransitive process verbs	不及物變化動詞	破、感冒、壞、死
Vpt	transitive process verbs	及物變化動詞	忘記、變成、丟
Vp-sep	intransitive process verbs, separable	不及物變化離合詞	結婚、生病、畢業

Default Values of the Symbols

Symbols	Default values
V	action, transitive
Vs	state, intransitive
Vp	process, intransitive
V-sep	separable, intransitive

1 上課了。
Shàngkè le.
Let's begin the class.

2 請打開書。
Qǐng dǎkāi shū.
Open your book.

3 請看第五頁。
Qǐng kàn dì wǔ yè.
Please see page 5.

4 我說，你們聽。
Wǒ shuō, nǐmen tīng.
I'll speak, you listen.

5 請跟我說。
Qǐng gēn wǒ shuō.
Please repeat after me.

6 請再說 / 念一次。
Qǐng zài shuō/niàn yí cì.
Please say it again.

7 請回答。
Qǐng huídá.
Please answer my question.

8 請問，這個字怎麼念 / 寫？
Qǐngwèn, zhè ge zì zěnme niàn/xiě?
How do you pronounce/spell this word?

9 對了！
Duì le!
Right! Correct!

10 不對。
Bú duì.
Wrong. Incorrect.

11 請念對話。
Qǐng niàn duìhuà.
Read the dialogue, please.

12 請看黑板。
Qǐng kàn hēibǎn.
Look at the board, please.

13 懂不懂？
Dǒng bù dǒng?
Do you understand?

14 懂了！
Dǒng le!
Yes, I/we understand.

15 有沒有問題？
Yǒu méi yǒu wèntí?
Any question?

16 很好！
Hěn hǎo!
Very good!

17 下課。
Xiàkè.
The class is over.

李明華

Lǐ Mínghuá

Li Ming-hua is from Taipei, Taiwan.
Male. Age 32. Single.

He works in a bank. He has worked in Vietnam for 6 months and is an acquaintance of Yue-mei Chen's father, who entrusted the responsibility of taking care of his daughter to Ming-hua. They met at the airport.

陳月美

Chén Yuèměi

Chen Yue-mei is from Hanoi, Vietnam.
Female. Age 22.

She traveled to Taiwan with her father's friend, Wang Kai-wen. They were picked up at the airport by Ming-hua, her father's Taiwanese acquaintance.
She is a student. Ru-yu and An-tong are her classmates.

白如玉

Bái Rúyù

Bai Ru-yu is from New York, USA.
Female. Age 21.

She is a student. Yue-mei and An-tong are her classmates.

馬安同

Mǎ Āntóng

Ma An-tong is from Tegucigalpa, Republic of Honduras.
Male. Age 22.

He is a student. Yue-mei and Ru-yu are his classmates.
He is Yi-jun's language exchange partner and Yi-jun is his best friend in Taiwan.

張怡君

Zhāng Yíjūn

Zhang Yi-jun is a Taiwanese college student.
Female. Age 20.

Her college is situated in a mountain in Hualien. She met An-tong on a trip. She is a language exchange partner of An-tong.

田中誠一

Tiánzhōng Chéngyī

Tianzhong Chengyi is from Tokyo, Japan.
Male. Age 30. Single.

He works in Taiwan as an expatriate of a Japanese motor company. Besides working, he is also learning Chinese in a language center. He is in the same class with Yue-mei, Ru-yu, and An-tong and he happens to be Li Ming-hua's client. Tianzhong's girlfriend is coming to Taiwan and he wants to show her around.

目 次 Contents

Contents

LESSON 11

第十一課

我要租房子
I Would Like to Rent a Place

學習目標 Learning Objectives

Topic: 租房子 Renting a Place

- Learning to talk about renting a place to live.
- Learning to talk about environment of a room or a house.
- Learning to make requests, e.g., to one's landlord.

我要租房子

I Would Like to Rent a Place

對話一 Dialogue 1 11-01 11-A

如 玉	：	林先生，你好，我是白如玉，來看房子。
房 東	：	白小姐，妳好，請進。
房 東	：	這裡是客廳，廚房在左邊，右邊有浴室。
如 玉	：	房子很不錯。
房 東	：	這裡很方便，附近有超市和捷運站，走路五分鐘就到了。
如 玉	：	現在有人住嗎？
房 東	：	有。還有兩間空房間，一間是套房，一間不是。
如 玉	：	我想看套房。房間裡面可以上網嗎？
房 東	：	可以。妳覺得這間房間怎麼樣？妳想租嗎？
如 玉	：	我回去想想，再打電話給你。

課文拼音 Text in Pinyin

Rúyù : Lín Xiānshēng, nǐ hǎo, wǒ shì Bái Rúyù, lái kàn fángzi.

Fángdōng : Bái Xiǎojiě, nǐ hǎo, qǐng jìn.

Fángdōng : Zhèlǐ shì kètīng, chúfáng zài zuǒbiān, yòubiān yǒu yùshì.

Rúyù : Fángzi hěn búcuò.

Fángdōng : Zhèlǐ hěn fāngbiàn, fùjìn yǒu chāoshì hàn jiéyùnzhàn, zǒulù wǔ fēnzhōng
         jiù dào le.

Rúyù : Xiànzài yǒu rén zhù ma?

Fángdōng : Yǒu. Hái yǒu liǎng jiān kōng fángjiān, yì jiān shì tàofáng, yì jiān bú shì.

Rúyù : Wǒ xiǎng kàn tàofáng. Fángjiān lǐmiàn kěyǐ shàngwǎng ma?

Fángdōng : Kěyǐ. Nǐ juéde zhè jiān fángjiān zěnmeyàng? Nǐ xiǎng zū ma?

Rúyù : Wǒ huíqù xiǎngxiǎng, zài dǎ diànhuà gěi nǐ.

課文英譯 Text in English

Ruyu : Hi, Mr. Lin. I am Bai Ruyu. I'm here to look at the house.

Landlord : Miss Bai, how are you? Please come in.

Landlord : This is the living room. The kitchen is to the left. The bathroom is to the right.

Ruyu : The place is nice.

Landlord : It is conveniently located. Nearby, there are a supermarket and an MRT station.
          Walk five minutes and you're there.

Ruyu : Does anyone live here now?

Landlord : Yes. There are still two vacant rooms. One is a suite (a room with a bath)
          and the other one is not.

Ruyu : I'd like to take a look at the suite. Can you access the internet from the room?

Landlord : Yes. What do you think of this room? Do you want to rent it?

Ruyu : Let me go back and think about it. I will call you again.

生詞一 Vocabulary 1 🎧 11-02

Vocabulary

1	租	zū	ㄗㄨ	(V)	to rent
2	房東	fángdōng	ㄈㄤˊ ㄉㄨㄥ	(N)	landlord
3	客廳	kètīng	ㄎㄜˋ ㄊㄧㄥ	(N)	living room
4	廚房	chúfáng	ㄔㄨˊ ㄈㄤˊ	(N)	kitchen
5	左邊	zuǒbiān	ㄗㄨㄛˇ ㄅㄧㄢ	(N)	left (side)
6	右邊	yòubiān	ㄧㄡˋ ㄅㄧㄢ	(N)	right (side)
7	浴室	yùshì	ㄩˋ ㄕˋ	(N)	bathroom
8	超市	chāoshì	ㄔㄠ ㄕˋ	(N)	supermarket
9	走路	zǒulù	ㄗㄡˇ ㄌㄨˋ	(V-sep)	to walk
10	分鐘	fēnzhōng	ㄈㄣ ㄓㄨㄥ	(M)	measure word for minutes
11	就	jiù	ㄐㄧㄡˋ	(Adv)	only, merely
12	到	dào	ㄉㄠˋ	(Vp)	arrive
13	間	jiān	ㄐㄧㄢ	(M)	measure word for houses, rooms, etc.
14	空	kōng	ㄎㄨㄥ	(Vs)	vacant, empty
15	房間	fángjiān	ㄈㄤˊ ㄐㄧㄢ	(N)	room
16	套房	tàofáng	ㄊㄠˋ ㄈㄤˊ	(N)	suite, studio
17	回去	huíqù	ㄏㄨㄟˊ ㄑㄩˋ	(Vi)	to go back, to return
18	想	xiǎng	ㄒㄧㄤˇ	(V)	to think
19	再	zài	ㄗㄞˋ	(Adv)	and then
20	電話	diànhuà	ㄉㄧㄢˋ ㄏㄨㄚˋ	(N)	telephone
21	給	gěi	ㄍㄟˇ	(Prep)	to

Names

22	林	Lín	ㄌㄧㄣˊ		Chinese last name, common in Taiwan

Phrases

23	打電話	dǎ diànhuà	ㄉㄚˇ ㄉㄧㄢˋ ㄏㄨㄚˋ		to make a phone call

對話二 Dialogue 2 11-03 AR 11-B

如　玉：喂，房東先生，你好，我是白如玉，你收到我的房租了嗎？

房　東：我已經收到了，謝謝。妳習慣了嗎？

如　玉：習慣了。可是，有一個問題，熱水器的水好像不熱。

房　東：今天我會去看看。妳什麼時候有空？晚上可以嗎？

如　玉：不好意思，今天晚上我有事。

房　東：沒關係，明天下午呢？

如　玉：好，我在家等你。

房　東：那我明天下午兩點到。還有問題嗎？

如　玉：我想買電視。請問可以幫我裝有線電視嗎？

房　東：可以，不過妳得自己付錢。

如　玉：好的，謝謝你。

課文拼音 Text in Pinyin

Rúyù : Wéi, Fángdōng xiānshēng, nǐ hǎo, wǒ shì Bái Rúyù, nǐ shōudào wǒ de fángzū le ma?

Fángdōng : Wǒ yǐjīng shōudào le, xièxie. Nǐ xíguàn le ma?

Rúyù : Xíguàn le. Kěshì, yǒu yí ge wèntí, rèshuǐqì de shuǐ hǎoxiàng bú rè.

Fángdōng : Jīntiān wǒ huì qù kànkàn. Nǐ shénme shíhòu yǒu kòng? Wǎnshàng kěyǐ ma?

Rúyù : Bùhǎo yìsi, jīntiān wǎnshàng wǒ yǒu shì.

Fángdōng : Méi guānxi, míngtiān xiàwǔ ne?

Rúyù : Hǎo, wǒ zài jiā děng nǐ.

Fángdōng : Nà wǒ míngtiān xiàwǔ liǎngdiǎn dào. Hái yǒu wèntí ma?

Rúyù : Wǒ xiǎng mǎi diànshì. Qǐngwèn kěyǐ bāng wǒ zhuāng yǒuxiàn diànshì ma?

Fángdōng : Kěyǐ, búguò nǐ děi zìjǐ fùqián.

Rúyù : Hǎode, xièxie nǐ.

課文英譯 Text in English

Ruyu : Hello, Mr. Landlord. This is Bai Ruyu. Have you received my rent?

Landlord : I have received it. Thank you. Are you accustomed (to living there)?

Ruyu : Yes. But there is a problem. The water from the water heater doesn't seem to be hot.

Landlord : I will go check it out today. When are you free? Would tonight be okay?

Ruyu : I am sorry. I've got something to do this evening.

Landlord : That is alright. How about tomorrow afternoon?

Ruyu : Okay. I will wait for you at home.

Landlord : I will be there at two. Are there any other problems?

Ruyu : I want to buy a television. Could I trouble you put in cable for me?

Landlord : Yes, but you will have to pay for it yourself.

Ruyu : Fine. Thank you.

生詞二 Vocabulary 2 11-04

Vocabulary

1	喂	wéi	ㄨㄟˊ	(Ptc)	a particle used in addressing people, especially over the phone
2	房租	fángzū	ㄈㄤˊ ㄗㄨ	(N)	rent (for a room or a house)
3	已經	yǐjīng	ㄧˇ ㄐㄧㄥ	(Adv)	already
4	習慣	xíguàn	ㄒㄧˊ ㄍㄨㄢˋ	(Vs)	to get settled down, to get used to
5	問題	wèntí	ㄨㄣˋ ㄊㄧˊ	(N)	problem, question
6	熱水器	rèshuǐqì	ㄖㄜˋ ㄕㄨㄟˇ ㄑㄧˋ	(N)	water heater
7	好像	hǎoxiàng	ㄏㄠˇ ㄒㄧㄤˋ	(Adv)	to seem to be, to appear to be (often used to take the edge off of a comment)
8	會	huì	ㄏㄨㄟˋ	(Vaux)	will
9	等	děng	ㄉㄥˇ	(V)	to wait for
10	那	nà	ㄋㄚˋ	(Ptc)	then, in that case
11	裝	zhuāng	ㄓㄨㄤ	(V)	to install
12	不過	búguò	ㄅㄨˊ ㄍㄨㄛˋ	(Conj)	however, but
13	付	fù	ㄈㄨˋ	(V)	to pay

Phrases

14	收到	shōudào	ㄕㄡ ㄉㄠˋ	to receive
15	不好意思	bùhǎo yìsi	ㄅㄨˋ ㄏㄠˇ ㄧˋ ㄙ	sorry
16	沒關係	méi guānxi	ㄇㄟˊ ㄍㄨㄢ ㄒㄧ	Not a problem.
17	有線電視	yǒuxiàn diànshì	ㄧㄡˇ ㄒㄧㄢˋ ㄉㄧㄢˋ ㄕˋ	cable TV

文法 Grammar

I. To Come to Do Something with 來 lái  11-05

Function: '來 *lái* + VP' indicates the subject's intention of coming over to do something.

1. 我來學中文。
2. 他來打籃球。
3. 我和朋友來逛夜市。

Structures: Negation markers, auxiliary verbs, or adverbs are placed before the first verbal element 來 *lái*.

Negation:

1. 我明天有事不來上課。
2. 她不跟我來看電影。
3. 我很忙,不來幫你裝有線電視了。

Questions:

1. 他不來吃晚飯嗎?
2. 你們常來游泳嗎?
3. 你要來參觀故宮博物院嗎?

Usage: The function of '來 + VP' in this lesson is the same as that of '去 + VP' in Lesson 3. The only difference is the direction of the subject's action, 來 towards and 去 away from the speaker's location.

1. 我星期四 來 / 去 上書法課。
2. 我妹妹不想 來 / 去 吃牛肉麵。

練習 Exercise

Complete sentences with 來 ＋ VP.

①

下個星期六我們可以一起

＿＿＿＿＿＿＿＿＿。

②

這個週末，

我不 ＿＿＿＿＿＿＿＿＿。

③

你有空的時候，

常 ＿＿＿＿＿＿＿＿ 嗎？

④

貓空的風景很美，我有時候

＿＿＿＿＿，有時候 ＿＿＿＿＿＿。

II. Sooner Than Expected with 就 jiù   11-06

拼音、英譯 p.15

Function: When 就 *jiù* refers to time or place, the event being discussed takes place sooner than expected.

① 學校很近。走路十分鐘就到了。
② 那個地方不遠。很快就到了。
③ 他等一下就來。

Structures: 就 *jiù* often co-occurs with the sentence-final 了 *le*. See above. The sentences mean the same with or without 了.

Usage: 就 *jiù* is a high-frequency adverb, which has various functions and meanings. It can be used in a single sentence, as introduced in this lesson, and it can be a linking adverb as introduced in Lesson 9, connecting S2 to S1.

練習 Exercise

Complete the following sentences by using 就, plus 了 when appropriate.

① 那個地方，坐捷運去比較快，十分鐘 _____。

② 他今天沒課，下午三點 _____。

③ 她剛打電話給我，她說老師等一下 _____。

④ 今天是三月十二號，他三月十五號 _____。（回國）

III. Existential Subject with 有 yǒu 11-07    拼音、英譯 p.15

Function: 有 *yǒu* introduces the existence of an indefinite subject. The following VP in the sentence describes what the subject does.

① 有人住這裡。

② 有兩個學生來找你。

③ 早上有一個小姐打電話給你。

④ 昨天有一個先生來裝有線電視。

⑤ 有一個人在外面唱歌。

Structures: The subject in Chinese is usually a definite noun. If the subject is indefinite, it needs to be preceded by 有 *yǒu*.

Negation: 有 is always negated with 沒.

① 這間沒有人住。

② 沒有人要跟我去逛夜市。

③ 沒有學生要去故宮。

✐ Questions:

1 有人在裡面看書嗎？

2 有沒有人想去 KTV 唱歌？

3 有沒有人要跟我一起去花蓮玩？

4 有沒有人不喜歡吃日本麵？

Usage: "有 + NP + 在 + location" is equivalent in meaning to "location + 有 + NP": 地上有一支手機。Dìshàng yǒu yì zhī shǒujī, 'The floor has a cellphone on it,' and 有一支手機在地上。Yǒu yì zhī shǒujī zài dìshàng, 'There is a cellphone on the floor.' However, the focuses of the two sentences are different. In the first one, the focus is on "the cellphone", while in the second one, the focus is "the floor". Compare the following dialogues.

1 A：地上有一支手機。　　B：是誰的？

2 A：有一支手機在地上。　　B：地上？為什麼在地上？

練習 Exercise

Rearrange the order of the following into existential subject sentences.

1 一個學生　有　唱歌　在
　　　①　　　②　③　④

＿＿＿＿＿＿＿＿＿＿＿＿＿＿＿＿＿＿＿＿。

2 有　照相　一個小姐　在大樓前面
　　①　②　　③　　　　④

＿＿＿＿＿＿＿＿＿＿＿＿＿＿＿＿＿＿＿＿。

3 人　有　打電話　給你　今天早上
　①　②　　③　　④　　　⑤

＿＿＿＿＿＿＿＿＿＿＿＿＿＿＿＿＿＿＿＿。

4 來接我　明天　有　人　嗎
　　①　　　②　　③　④　⑤

＿＿＿＿＿＿＿＿＿＿＿＿＿＿＿＿＿＿？

IV. Different Types of 會 huì  11-08

Usage: There are two different types of 會 *huì*. The first one, as presented in Lesson 5, refers to "acquired skills". The second one, in this lesson, refers to "possiblity or likelihood".

❶ 他會做飯。（會₁）
❷ 我不會打籃球。（會₁）
❸ 我明天會去看看他。（會₂）
❹ 他明天不會去上書法課。（會₂）

練習 Exercise

Please identify the types of 會 *huì* in the following sentences, and mark them accordingly.

	會 1	會 2
A. 我姐姐「會」做甜點了。	( )	( )
B. 他等一下就「會」去看電影了。	( )	( )
C. 我弟弟已經「會」騎機車了。	( )	( )
D. 我跟女朋友明天不「會」去 KTV。	( )	( )
E. 他「會」寫書法，可是寫得不太好。	( )	( )

V. Omitting Nouns at 2nd Mention 11-09

Function: In Chinese, old information that has been mentioned before or that is understood from the context is often omitted later. A pronoun that is omitted is called a "zero pronoun".

Structures: The most frequently omitted elements are the subject and the object.

1. subject predictable from contexts

(1) ∅ 請進！（L2）

(2) [store clerk asking customer]
∅ 要買什麼？
請問 ∅ 外帶還是內用？（L4）

(3) [A calling B]
今天晚上 ∅ 要一起吃晚飯嗎？（L3）

(4) ∅ 聽說臺灣有很多小吃。（L5）

2. subject previously mentioned

(1) 我姓王，∅ 叫開文。（L1）

(2) 我常打籃球，∅ 也常踢足球。（L3）

3. object previously mentioned

昨天朋友給我一個芒果，我不想吃 ∅。

練習 Exercise

There are omissions in the following dialogues. Please identify the omitted elements.

1. **(1)** 要是那時候我有空，（　　　）就跟你們一起去。（L9）

   (2) 我以前不喜歡吃水果，（　　　）現在很喜歡了。（L10）

2. **(1)** A: 那種手機很好，我哥哥有一支（　　　）。

   B:（　　　）貴不貴？一支（　　　）賣多少錢？（L4）

   (2) a. 我們　b. 牛肉麵

   A：牛肉麵真的這麼好吃嗎？

   B：是的。牛肉好吃，湯也好喝。

   A：（　　　）這麼好吃，我想吃吃看。

   B：明天我們去吃。（　）一定要點大碗的（　）。（L4）

3. a. 我　b. 你們　c. 我們

   安同：我想跟朋友去玩。

   田中：不錯啊，（　　　）去什麼地方？

安同：花蓮。（　　　）聽說那裡的風景非常漂亮。

田中：我也聽說。放假的時候，你常去旅行嗎？

安同：不一定，（　　　）有時候在家寫功課，有時候出去玩。

田中：你們什麼時候去花蓮？

安同：（　　　）這個星期六下午去。

田中：（　　　）去玩多久？

安同：（　　　）大概玩四、五天。（L9）

語法例句拼音與英譯
Grammar Examples in Pinyin and English

I. To Come to Do Something with 來 lái

Function:

1. Wǒ lái xué Zhōngwén.
2. Tā lái dǎ lánqiú.
3. Wǒ hàn péngyǒu lái guàng yèshì.

Function:

1. I've come to study Chinese.
2. He came to play baseketball.
3. My friend and I came to wander around the night market.

Structures:

✏️ **Negation:**

1. Wǒ míngtiān yǒu shì bù lái shàngkè.
2. Tā bù gēn wǒ lái kàn diànyǐng.
3. Wǒ hěn máng, bù lái bāng nǐ zhuāng yǒuxiàn diànshì le.

Structures:

✏️ **Negation:**

1. I have something to do tomorrow. I won't be coming to class.
2. She did not come with me to see a movie.
3. I am very busy. I can't come put cable television in for you.

✏️ **Questions:**

1. Tā bù lái chī wǎnfàn ma?
2. Nǐmen cháng lái yóuyǒng ma?
3. Nǐ yào lái cānguān Gùgōng Bówùyuàn ma?

✏️ **Questions:**

1. He's not coming to eat dinner?
2. Do you often come to swim?
3. Are you coming to visit the Palace Museum?

Usage:

1 Wǒ xīngqísì lái/qù shàng shūfǎ kè.

2 Wǒ mèimei bù xiǎng lái/qù chī niúròu miàn.

Usage:

1 I come/go take calligraphy classes on Thursdays.

2 My sister doesn't want to come/go eat beef noodles.

II. Sooner Than Expected with 就 jiù

Function:

1 Xuéxiào hěn jìn. Zǒulù shí fēnzhōng jiù dào le.

2 Nà ge dìfāng bù yuǎn. Hěn kuài jiù dào le.

3 Tā děng yíxià jiù lái.

Function:

1 The school is close. Walking only ten minutes will get you there.

2 That place is not far. You'll get there very quickly.

3 He will be here in a bit.

III. Existential Subject with 有 yǒu

Function:

1 Yǒu rén zhù zhèlǐ.

2 Yǒu liǎng ge xuéshēng lái zhǎo nǐ.

3 Zǎoshàng yǒu yí ge xiǎojiě dǎ diànhuà gěi nǐ.

4 Zuótiān yǒu yí ge xiānshēng lái zhuāng yǒuxiàn diànshì.

5 Yǒu yí ge rén zài wàimiàn chànggē.

Function:

1 Somebody is living here.

2 There are two students looking for you.

3 This morning some woman phoned you.

4 Some man came yesterday to install cable TV.

5 Someone is singing outside.

Structures:

✏ Negation:

1 Zhè jiān méi yǒu rén zhù.

2 Méi yǒu rén yào gēn wǒ qù guàng yèshì.

3 Méi yǒu xuéshēng yào qù Gùgōng.

Structures:

✏ Negation:

1 There is no one living in this room.

2 Nobody wants to go walk around the night market with me.

3 None of the students wants to visit the Palace Museum.

Questions:

1. Yǒu rén zài lǐmiàn kànshū ma?
2. Yǒu méi yǒu rén xiǎng qù KTV chànggē?
3. Yǒu méi yǒu rén yào gēn wǒ yìqǐ qù Huālián wán?
4. Yǒu méi yǒu rén bù xǐhuān chī Rìběn miàn?

Usage:

1. A: Dìshàng yǒu yì zhī shǒujī.
   B: Shì shéi de?
2. A: Yǒu yì zhī shǒujī zài dìshàng.
   B: Dìshàng? Wèishénme zài dìshàng?

Questions:

1. Is there someone inside studying?
2. Is there anyone who wants to go to KTV to sing?
3. Is there anyone who wants to go to Hualien with me?
4. Is there anyone who doesn't like to eat Japanese noodles?

Usage:

1. A: There is a cellphone on the floor.
   B: Whose is it?
2. A: There is a cellphone on the floor.
   B: On the floor? Why on the floor?

IV. Different Types of 會 huì

Usage:

1. Tā huì zuòfàn.
2. Wǒ bú huì dǎ lánqiú.
3. Wǒ míngtiān huì qù kànkàn tā.
4. Tā míngtiān bú huì qù shàng shūfǎ kè.

Usage:

1. He knows how to cook.
2. I don't know how to play basketball.
3. I will visit him tomorrow.
4. He won't go to calligraphy class tomorrow.

V. Omitting Nouns at 2nd Mention

Structures:

1. subject predictable from contexts
   (1) Qǐngjìn! (L2)
   (2) Yào mǎi shénme?
       Qǐngwèn, wàidài háishì nèiyòng? (L4)
   (3) Jīntiān wǎnshàng yào yìqǐ chī wǎnfàn ma? (L3)
   (4) Tīngshuō Táiwān yǒu hěn duō xiǎochī. (L5)

2. subject previously mentioned
   (1) Wǒ xìng Wáng, jiào Kāiwén. (L1)
   (2) Wǒ cháng dǎ lánqiú, yě cháng tī zúqiú. (L3)

3. object previously mentioned
   Zuótiān péngyǒu gěi wǒ yí ge mángguǒ, wǒ bù xiǎng chī.

Structures:

1. subject predictable from contexts
   (1) (You) please come in. (L2)
   (2) What would (you) like to buy?
       Excuse me, is this for here or to go? (L4)
   (3) Shall (we) eat dinner together tonight? (L3)
   (4) (I've) heard that Taiwan has lots of (different kinds of) light repasts. (L5)

2. subject previously mentioned
   (1) I am surnamed Wang. (I) am called Kaiwen. (L1)
   (2) I often play basketball and (I) often play football. (L3)

3. object previously mentioned
   Yesterday, a friend gave me a mango. I don't want to eat (it).

 **Classroom Activities**

I. Life in Taiwan / Photo Journal

Goal: Learning to use indefinite subjects to describe events.

Task: 安同 took a walk in his neighborhood on Sunday and took a few photos. He plans to upload them to Facebook. Please help him write down captions for each one. Describe where the actions took place.

❶ 有一個學生在學校打籃球。

❷

❸

❹

II. Where I Live

Goal: Learning to talk about the environment of a room or house.

Task: Pair up with a classmate and describe your current residence or your residence back in your home country. As you listen to your partner, draw a floor plan of their house and label each room.

III. Story-telling

Goal: Learning to comprehend a passage and add things to it.

Task: Form groups of two or three. Read the following story and complete it with your partners. Read the completed story to the class. Evaluate each group's work.

> 　　李大同的女朋友昨天已經回國了。現在他一個人在家,他想,今天有一個很好看的網球比賽,可是現在十一點半了,比賽已經結束了。他不知道要做什麼,所以想去看看他爸爸媽媽,他爸媽的家很近,走路五分鐘就到了。他打電話給他爸媽,他爸媽說,他們去旅行,不在家。現在,李大同不知道要做什麼,…(請幫他想想吧!)
>
> _____
>
> _____
>
> _____

IV. For Rent Ads

Goal: Learning to understand rental advertisements.

Task: You and your friend see the rent ad below. Carry out a discussion based on the following questions.

租

近捷運站、超市、學校
兩套衛浴，有廚房
冰箱、網路、有線電視一應俱全
月租一萬五，不包水電

地址：師大路八巷六號二樓
意者請電王太太 02-73889012
0988123456

❶ 租這個房子一個月要多少錢？

❷ 租這個房子，可以做飯嗎？

❸ 要是我想看房子，應該打電話給誰？打哪個電話？

❹ 什麼是「衛浴」？

❺ 你現在住的房子比這個房子好嗎？

❻ 要是你想租房子，你會租這個地方嗎？為什麼？

V. Something's Wrong with My Room

Goal: Learning to make requests, e.g., to your landlord.

Task: You have just started renting a place, but you have discovered that there is something wrong with the internet and the kitchen has no hot running water. Call your landlord, tell him / her of the problems, and ask him / her to take care of them. (Have a classmate role play the landlord.)

_____

_____

_____

_____

_____

_____

_____

_____

文化 *Bits of Chinese Culture*

Renting a Place in Taiwan

Though it is possible to find rental apartments through real estate agents, in Taiwan, it is more common for landlords to rent their own places. Renting a place in Taiwan is very much a free market. In other words, while there are going prices for renting apartments, the final amount is determined by the landlord and it is possible to bargain the rent down. Therefore, it is best to shop around and haggle with the landlord to get a better price. Once an agreement is reached and written down on a lease, it has legal effect. Also in Taiwan, application fees or background screening fees are not necessary. However, the landlord might ask for a deposit of up to two months' rent, but prepayment of the final month's rent is not practiced.

▲ Rental ads on bulletin boards   ▲ Rental contract

Self-Assessment Checklist

I can talk about renting a place to live.

20%　　40%　　60%　　80%　　100%

I can talk about environment of a room or a house.

20%　　40%　　60%　　80%　　100%

I can make requests to someone, e.g., to my landlord.

20%　　40%　　60%　　80%　　100%

第十二課

你計畫在臺灣學多久的中文？
How Long Do You Plan to Study Chinese in Taiwan?

學習目標 Learning Objectives

Topic: 學習、工作 **Study, Work**

· Learning to discuss study plans and future plans.

· Learning to talk about sequences of events.

· Learning to describe past actions and experience.

LESSON 12

你計畫在臺灣學多久的中文？

How Long Do You Plan to Study Chinese in Taiwan?

田　　中：安同，你計畫在臺灣學多久的中文？

安　　同：五年。

田　　中：為什麼要這麼久的時間？

安　　同：我先在語言中心念一年，再念四年大學，
　　　　　所以需要五年。

田　　中：這得花不少錢！

安　　同：對，不過我有獎學金。要是成績不好，
　　　　　就沒獎學金了。你呢？

田　　中：我的學費是公司替我付的。

安　　同：你打算學多久呢？

田	中	：大概兩年，是公司決定的。
安	同	：希望我以後也可以到這麼好的公司上班。
田	中	：我又要上班，又要念書，真的很累。
安	同	：我們一起加油吧！

課文拼音 Text in Pinyin

Tiánzhōng	: Āntóng, nǐ jìhuà zài Táiwān xué duō jiǔ de Zhōngwén?
Āntóng	: Wǔ nián.
Tiánzhōng	: Wèishénme yào zhème jiǔ de shíjiān?
Āntóng	: Wǒ xiān zài yǔyán zhōngxīn niàn yì nián, zài niàn sì nián dàxué, suǒyǐ xūyào wǔ nián.
Tiánzhōng	: Zhè děi huā bù shǎo qián!
Āntóng	: Duì, búguò wǒ yǒu jiǎngxuéjīn. Yàoshì chéngjī bù hǎo, jiù méi jiǎngxuéjīn le. Nǐ ne?
Tiánzhōng	: Wǒ de xuéfèi shì gōngsī tì wǒ fù de.
Āntóng	: Nǐ dǎsuàn xué duō jiǔ ne?
Tiánzhōng	: Dàgài liǎng nián, shì gōngsī juédìng de.
Āntóng	: Xīwàng wǒ yǐhòu yě kěyǐ dào zhème hǎo de gōngsī shàngbān.
Tiánzhōng	: Wǒ yòu yào shàngbān, yòu yào niànshū, zhēnde hěn lèi.
Āntóng	: Wǒmen yìqǐ jiāyóu ba!

課文英譯 Text in English

Tianzhong	: Antong, how long do you plan to study Chinese in Taiwan?
Antong	: Five years.
Tianzhong	: Why such a long time?

Antong   : I am going to study for a year at the language center, then study at university for four years, so I need five years.

Tianzhong   : That's going to cost a lot of money.

Antong   : That's right, but I have a scholarship. If my grades are poor, I will lose it. And you?

Tianzhong   : My tuition is paid by my company for me.

Antong   : And how long do you plan to study?

Tianzhong   : Probably two years. My company will decide.

Antong   : I hope later I can work at such a good company.

Tianzhong   : I have to both work and study. It is exhausting.

Antong   : Let's keep up the good work.

生詞一 Vocabulary 12-02

Vocabulary

1	計畫	jìhuà	ㄐㄧˋ ㄏㄨㄚˋ	(V)	to plan to
2	年	nián	ㄋㄧㄢˊ	(M)	measure word for year
3	久	jiǔ	ㄐㄧㄡˇ	(Vs)	long (time)
4	時間	shíjiān	ㄕˊ ㄐㄧㄢ	(N)	time
5	先	xiān	ㄒㄧㄢ	(Adv)	first
6	念	niàn	ㄋㄧㄢˋ	(V)	to study
7	大學	dàxué	ㄉㄚˋ ㄒㄩㄝˊ	(N)	university
8	需要	xūyào	ㄒㄩ ㄧㄠˋ	(Vst)	to need
9	花	huā	ㄏㄨㄚ	(V)	to spend (time or money)
10	獎學金	jiǎngxuéjīn	ㄐㄧㄤˇ ㄒㄩㄝˊ ㄐㄧㄣ	(N)	scholarship
11	成績	chéngjī	ㄔㄥˊ ㄐㄧ	(N)	grades
12	學費	xuéfèi	ㄒㄩㄝˊ ㄈㄟˋ	(N)	tuition
13	公司	gōngsī	ㄍㄨㄥ ㄙ	(N)	company
14	替	tì	ㄊㄧˋ	(Prep)	for, on behalf of
15	希望	xīwàng	ㄒㄧ ㄨㄤˋ	(Vst)	to hope

16	以後	yǐhòu	ㄧˇ ㄏㄡˋ	(N)	in the future
17	到	dào	ㄉㄠˋ	(V)	to go/come to
18	上班	shàngbān	ㄕㄤˋ ㄅㄢ	(V-sep)	to go to work
19	念書	niànshū	ㄋㄧㄢˋ ㄕㄨ	(V-sep)	to study
20	累	lèi	ㄌㄟˋ	(Vs)	tired

Phrases

| 21 | 語言中心 | yǔyán zhōngxīn | ㄩˇ ㄧㄢˊ ㄓㄨㄥ ㄒㄧㄣ | | language center |
| 22 | 加油 | jiāyóu | ㄐㄧㄚ ㄧㄡˊ | | keep up the good work |

對話二 Dialogue 2 🎧 12-03 🄰🄡 12-B

月　美：田中，你是什麼時候來臺灣工作的？

田　中：去年，我已經在臺灣工作一年了。

月　美：為什麼你們公司要替你付學費？

田　中：因為我們公司跟臺灣人做生意。老闆希望我們
　　　　都會說中文。

月　美：我覺得你們公司真好。

田　中：對了，妳回國以後，打算做什麼？

月　美：我回國以後，也想找個有機會說中文的工作。

田　中：不錯，這樣的工作在你們國家好找嗎？

月　美：不知道好不好找，我試試看。

田　中：要是難找呢？

月　美：那麼我再來臺灣學中文。

田　中：太好了！那我們就可以再見面了。

課文拼音 Text in Pinyin

Yuèměi　　 : Tiánzhōng, nǐ shì shénme shíhòu lái Táiwān gōngzuò de?

Tiánzhōng: Qùnián, wǒ yǐjīng zài Táiwān gōngzuò yì nián le.

Yuèměi　　 : Wèishénme nǐmen gōngsī yào tì nǐ fù xuéfèi?

Tiánzhōng: Yīnwèi wǒmen gōngsī gēn Táiwān rén zuò shēngyì. Lǎobǎn xīwàng wǒmen dōu huì shuō Zhōngwén.

Yuèměi　　 : Wǒ juéde nǐmen gōngsī zhēn hǎo.

Tiánzhōng: Duìle, nǐ huíguó yǐhòu, dǎsuàn zuò shénme?

Yuèměi　　 : Wǒ huíguó yǐhòu, yě xiǎng zhǎo ge yǒu jīhuì shuō Zhōngwén de gōngzuò.

Tiánzhōng: Búcuò, zhèyàng de gōngzuò zài nǐmen guójiā hǎo zhǎo ma?

Yuèměi　　 : Bù zhīdào hǎo bù hǎo zhǎo, wǒ shìshìkàn.

Tiánzhōng: Yàoshì nán zhǎo ne?

Yuèměi　　 : Nàme wǒ zài lái Táiwān xué Zhōngwén.

Tiánzhōng: Tài hǎo le! Nà wǒmen jiù kěyǐ zài jiànmiàn le.

課文英譯 Text in English

Yuemei : When did you come to Taiwan to work, Tianzhong?

Tianzhong: Last year. I have been working in Taiwan for a year.

Yuemei : Why does your company pay tuition for you?

Tianzhong: Because our company does business with Taiwanese. My boss wants us all to speak Chinese.

Yuemei : I think your company is really good.

Tianzhong: By the way, what do you plan to do when you go back to your country?

Yuemei : After I go back home, I would like to find a job (that gives me) opportunities to speak Chinese.

Tianzhong: Not a bad idea. Is that kind of job easy to find in your country?

Yuemei : I don't know if they are easy to find, but I am going to try.

Tianzhong: What if they are hard to find?

Yuemei : Then, I would come back to Taiwan to study Chinese.

Tianzhong: Great. That way we could see each other again.

生詞二 Vocabulary 2 12-04

Vocabulary

1	工作	gōngzuò	ㄍㄨㄥ ㄗㄨㄛˋ	(Vi)	to work
2	去年	qùnián	ㄑㄩˋ ㄋㄧㄢˊ	(N)	last year
3	做	zuò	ㄗㄨㄛˋ	(V)	to do, to engage in
4	生意	shēngyì	ㄕㄥ ㄧˋ	(N)	business
5	以後	yǐhòu	ㄧˇ ㄏㄡˋ	(N)	afterwards
6	好	hǎo	ㄏㄠˇ	(Vs)	easy to
7	找	zhǎo	ㄓㄠˇ	(V)	to look for
8	工作	gōngzuò	ㄍㄨㄥ ㄗㄨㄛˋ	(N)	job, work
9	這樣	zhèyàng	ㄓㄜˋ ㄧㄤˋ	(N)	this kind (of)
10	國家	guójiā	ㄍㄨㄛˊ ㄐㄧㄚ	(N)	country
11	試	shì	ㄕˋ	(Vi)	to try

12	難	nán	ㄋㄢˊ	(Vs)	hard to, difficult to
13	那麼	nàme	ㄋㄚˋ ㄇㄜ˙	(Ptc)	then
14	再	zài	ㄗㄞˋ	(Adv)	again

Phrases

| 15 | 試試看 | shìshìkàn | ㄕˋ ㄕˋ ㄎㄢˋ | | to give it a try,
to try and see what happens |

文法 Grammar

I. 先 xiān⋯，再 zài⋯ *first..., and then...* **12-05**  拼音、英譯 p.38

Function: This pattern presents the temporal sequence of two consecutive events.

① 弟弟打算先去旅行再找工作。
② 我想先吃晚飯再給媽媽打電話。
③ 他計畫在臺灣先學語言再念大學。

Usage: This pattern indicates the order of two events either in the past or future.

① 我昨天晚上先寫功課，再看電視。
② 我明天先去圖書館看書，再去超市買東西。

練習 Exercise

Complete the situations below based on the pictures given.

①

我每天先 ＿＿＿＿＿＿＿＿＿＿＿＿＿，
再 ＿＿＿＿＿＿＿＿＿＿＿＿＿。

2

他想先 _____，

再 _____。

3

我常先 _____，

再 _____。

4

我今天晚上要先 _____，

再 _____。

5

他們明天打算先去 _____，

再去 _____。

II. To Focus with 是 shì…的 de 12-06

拼音、英譯 p.38

Function: This pattern highlights one of the elements in a sentence in a past event and marks it as the focus/contrast, i.e., the main message of the sentence.

Structures:

1. In this pattern, the focus marker 是 is placed directly in front of the focused element and 的 is placed at the end of the sentence, i.e., Subject ＋ 是 ＋ Focus ＋ Activity ＋ 的.

   (1) 他是昨天晚上到臺灣的。　　**(2)** 他是在學校附近吃晚飯的。
   (3) 我是坐捷運來學校的。

2. The object in the sentence is often moved to the very front of the sentence.

   (1) 學費是公司替我付的。　　**(2)** 這支手機是在夜市買的。

3. The focused element can be the subject, the expression for time, place, manner, and occasionally the verb, but never the object.

   (1) 是我打電話給房東的。　　　　　　（subject）
   (2) 我是昨天晚上去看電影的。　　　　（time）
   (3) 他是在那家便利商店買咖啡的。　　（place）
   (4) 我是坐公車來上課的。　　　　　　（manner）
   BUT NOT, *我是這間房間最近租的。　　（object）

 **Negation:** The negation marker 不 *bú* always goes before 是 *shì*.

   ❶ 他不是今天早上去美國的。　　❷ 不是我打電話給房東的。
   ❸ 我不是在圖書館看書的。

Questions:

   ❶ 你是一個人來的嗎？　　❷ 他是坐高鐵去臺南的嗎？
   ❸ 你的房租是自己付的嗎？

Usage:

1. Sometimes 是 *shì* can be omitted in the 是…的 pattern.

   (1) 我（是）跟朋友一起來的。　　**(2)** 我（是）坐計程車來的。

2. This pattern can be used to ask a wh-question (*who, when, how, where*) about an event in the past, however, it does not work when "what" is the object.

   (1) 是誰打電話給你的？　　　　　　（who）

(2) 他是什麼時候來學校的？　　　（when）

(3) 你是怎麼去的？　　　　　　　（how）

(4) 你是在哪裡吃飯的？　　　　　（where）

　　*你是什麼東西看的？　　　　（object）

練習 Exercise

Based on the pictures given below, play out the A and B roles.

❶

A：他（是什麼時候）去學校的？

B：他是 ＿＿＿＿＿＿＿ 去學校的。

❷

A：（在哪裡？）

B：＿＿＿＿＿＿＿＿

❸

A：（怎麼去？）

B：＿＿＿＿＿＿＿＿

❹

A：（跟誰去？）

B：＿＿＿＿＿＿＿＿

❺

A：（學費誰付？）

B：＿＿＿＿＿＿＿＿

III. 以後 yǐhòu　*after...*　🎧 12-07　🔍 拼音、英譯 p.39

Function: In this lesson 以後 *yǐhòu* is basically a noun but covers two different functions. In Dialogue 1, it is used alone, just like a time word, meaning some time in the future. In Dialogue 2, it is used together with two events, connecting them sequentially, i.e., after A, B....

Structures:

Dialogue 1 Structure:

① 我們以後都得上班。

② 他們以後還要再到臺南去。

Dialogue 2 Structure:

① 回國以後，我要找個有機會說中文的工作。

② 來臺灣以後，我每星期上五天的中文課。

③ 我下課以後，常在圖書館上網。

練習 Exercise

Complete the following dialogues by using 以後 .

	學生 A（問）	學生 B（答）
1	你每天幾點吃晚飯？	我每天<u>七點半以後</u>吃晚飯。
2	我們什麼時候去吃晚飯？	＿＿＿＿＿＿＿＿＿＿＿。
3	你什麼時候回國？	＿＿＿＿＿＿＿＿＿＿。
4	你是什麼時候去圖書館的？	＿＿＿＿＿＿＿＿＿＿。
5	你是什麼時候學中文的？	＿＿＿＿＿＿＿＿＿＿。
6	他是什麼時候打電話給你的？	＿＿＿＿＿＿＿＿＿＿。
7	半年以後，你打算做什麼？	＿＿＿＿＿＿＿＿＿＿。
8	一個月以後，你要去旅行嗎？	＿＿＿＿＿＿＿＿＿＿。

	學生 A（問）	學生 B（答）
9	昨天你下課以後做什麼？	＿＿＿＿＿＿＿＿＿＿＿＿＿。
10	回國以後，你想做什麼？	＿＿＿＿＿＿＿＿＿＿＿＿＿。

IV. Special Meanings of 好 *hǎo*/ 難 *nán* + Verbs 12-08

Function:

1. When 好 or 難 combine with perception verbs, they become single words.

好吃	難吃
好喝	難喝
好看	難看
好聽	難聽

2. When they combine with action verbs, 好 means "easy to" and 難 "difficult/ hard to".

好學	難學
好寫	難寫
好做	難做
好找	難找

(1) 日本菜好吃也好看。 (2) 好工作很難找。

(3) 這個歌好聽也好唱。

Structures: Degree adverbs such as 很 *hěn* "very" can modify both structures given above .

❶ 我媽媽做的菜很好吃。 ❷ 有人覺得中文很難學。

✏ Negation:

1. With perception verb:
   (1) 便宜的咖啡不好喝。
   (2) 學校餐廳的菜不難吃。
   (3) 這個歌，唱得太慢不好聽。

2. With action verbs:
   (1) 這家店賣的小籠包不好做。
   (2) 老師常常說中文不難學。
   (3) 學校附近便宜的套房不好找。

✏ Questions:

1. With perception verbs:
   (1) 旅館老闆買的水果好吃嗎？
   (2) 你覺得那個電影好看不好看？
   (3) 點烏龍茶的那個先生唱歌唱得好聽嗎？

2. With action verbs:
   (1) 說中文的工作在你的國家好找嗎？
   (2) 又大又貴的房子好不好賣？
   (3) 老師今天教的甜點難不難學？

練習 Exercise

Comment on the pictures below using 好 / 難 + Verb combinations.

1

2
越南菜

3
日本茶

中國書法很好看。 ＿＿＿＿＿＿＿。 ＿＿＿＿＿＿＿。

4

5
爸爸 媽媽

6

＿＿＿＿＿＿＿。 中文 ＿＿＿＿＿＿＿。 ＿＿＿＿＿＿＿。

7

8

＿＿＿＿＿＿＿。 ＿＿＿＿＿＿＿。

I. 先 xiān… ，再 zài… *first..., and then...*

Function:

1. Dìdi dǎsuàn xiān qù lǚxíng zài zhǎo gōngzuò.
2. Wǒ xiǎng xiān chī wǎnfàn zài gěi māma dǎ diànhuà.
3. Tā jìhuà zài Táiwān xiān xué yǔyán zài niàn dàxué.

Usage:

1. Wǒ zuótiān wǎnshàng xiān xiě gōngkè, zài kàn diànshì.
2. Wǒ míngtiān xiān qù túshūguǎn kànshū, zài qù chāoshì mǎi dōngxi.

Function:

1. My brother plans to go traveling first and then look for a job.
2. I want to eat dinner first and then call my mom.
3. He plans to study language in Taiwan first and then go to college.

Usage:

1. Last night, I did my homework first and then watched TV.
2. Tomorrow, I'll study in the library first and then go shopping at the supermarket.

II. To Focus with 是 shì…的 de

Structures:

1. (1) Tā shì zuótiān wǎnshàng dào Táiwān de.
   (2) Tā shì zài xuéxiào fùjìn chī wǎnfàn de.
   (3) Wǒ shì zuò jiéyùn lái xuéxiào de.

2. (1) Xuéfèi shì gōngsī tì wǒ fù de.
   (2) Zhè zhī shǒujī shì zài yèshì mǎi de.

3. (1) Shì wǒ dǎ diànhuà gěi fángdōng de.
   (2) Wǒ shì zuótiān wǎnshàng qù kàn diànyǐng de.
   (3) Tā shì zài nà jiā biànlì shāngdiàn mǎi kāfēi de.
   (4) Wǒ shì zuò gōngchē lái shàngkè de.

Structures:

1. (1) It was last night that he arrived in Taiwan.
   (2) It was near the school that he had dinner.
   (3) It was by MRT that I came to school.

2. (1) It is the company that pays my tuition.
   (2) It was in the night market that I purchased this cellphone.

3. (1) It was I who called the landlord. (subject)
   (2) It was last night that I went to see a movie. (time)
   (3) It was in that convenience store that he bought coffee. (place)
   (4) It was by taking the bus that I came to class. (manner)

✏ **Negation:**

1 Tā búshì jīntiān zǎoshàng qù Měiguó de.
2 Búshì wǒ dǎ diànhuà gěi fángdōng de.
3 Wǒ búshì zài túshūguǎn kànshū de.

✏ **Questions:**

1 Nǐ shì yí ge rén lái de ma?

2 Tā shì zuò gāotiě qù Táinán de ma?

3 Nǐ de fángzū shì zìjǐ fù de ma?

Usage:

1. (1) Wǒ (shì) gēn péngyǒu yìqǐ lái de.

   (2) Wǒ (shì) zuò jìchéngchē lái de.

2. (1) Shì shéi dǎ diànhuà gěi nǐ de?
   (2) Tā shì shénme shíhòu lái xuéxiào de?
   (3) Nǐ shì zěnme qù de?
   (4) Nǐ shì zài nǎlǐ chīfàn de?

✏ **Negation:**

1 It was not this morning that he went to the United States.
2 It was not I who called the landlord.
3 It was not in the library that I studied.

✏ **Questions:**

1 Did you come alone? (Was it by yourself that you came?)
2 Did he go to Tainan by High Speed Rail? (Was it by High Speed Rail that he went to Tainan?)
3 Do you pay your own rent? (Is it you who pays your rent?)

Usage:

1. (1) I came with friends. (It was with friends that I came.)
   (2) I came by taxi. (It was by taxi that I came.)

2. (1) Who called you?
   (2) When did he come to school?
   (3) How did you go?
   (4) Where did you eat?

III. 以後 yǐhòu *after...*

Structures:

Dialogue 1 Structure:

1 Wǒmen yǐhòu dōu děi shàngbān.
2 Tāmen yǐhòu hái yào zài dào Táinán qù.

Dialogue 2 Structure:

1 Huíguó yǐhòu, wǒ yào zhǎo ge yǒu jīhuì shuō Zhōngwén de gōngzuò.

2 Lái Táiwān yǐhòu, wǒ měi xīngqí shàng wǔ tiān de Zhōngwén kè.

3 Wǒ xiàkè yǐhòu, cháng zài túshūguǎn shàngwǎng.

Structures:

Dialogue 1 Structure:

1 We will all have to work in the future.
2 They want to visit Tainan again in the future.

Dialogue 2 Structure:

1 After going back to my country, I want to look for a job that offers opportunities to speak Chinese.

2 After coming to Taiwan, I have been going to Chinese class five days a week.

3 After class, I often use the internet in the library.

IV. Special Meanings of 好 *hǎo* / 難 *nán* + Verbs

Function:

1.

hǎochī	nánchī
hǎohē	nánhē
hǎokàn	nánkàn
hǎotīng	nántīng

2.

hǎo xué	nán xué
hǎo xiě	nán xiě
hǎo zuò	nán zuò
hǎo zhǎo	nán zhǎo

(1) Rìběn cài hǎochī yě hǎokàn.

(2) Hǎo gōngzuò hěn nán zhǎo.
(3) Zhè ge gē hǎotīng yě hǎochàng.

Structures:

❶ Wǒ māma zuò de cài hěn hǎochī.

❷ Yǒu rén juéde Zhōngwén hěn nán xué.

✎ Negation:

1. (1) Piányí de kāfēi bù hǎohē.
   (2) Xuéxiào cāntīng de cài bù nánchī.
   (3) Zhè ge gē, chàng de tài màn bù hǎotīng.

2. (1) Zhè jiā diàn mài de xiǎolóngbāo bù hǎo zuò.
   (2) Lǎoshī chángcháng shuō Zhōngwén bù nán xué.
   (3) Xuéxiào fùjìn piányí de tàofáng bù hǎo zhǎo.

Function:

1.

nice to eat	not nice to eat
nice to drink	not nice to drink
nice-looking	not nice-looking, ugly
nice to listen to	not nice to listen to

2.

easy to learn	hard to learn
easy to write	hard to write
easy to do	hard to do
easy to find	hard to find

(1) Japanese food is both delicious and visually pleasing.
(2) Finding a good job is difficult.
(3) This song is both nice to listen to and easy to sing.

Structures:

❶ The food my mom makes is (very) delicious.
❷ Some people think that Chinese is (very) hard to learn.

✎ Negation:

1. (1) Cheap coffee doesn't taste good.
   (2) School cafeteria food tastes okay.
   (3) This song does not sound nice if sung too slowly.

2. (1) The xiaolongbao sold at this shop are hard to make.
   (2) The teacher often says that Chinese is not difficult to learn.
   (3) Suites near the school that are cheap to rent are hard to find.

✏️ **Questions:**

1. **(1)** Does the fruit bought by the hotel owner taste good?
   (2) Do you think that movie was good or bad?
   (3) Does the man who ordered Oolong tea sing well?

2. **(1)** Are jobs in which you speak Chinese easy to find in your country?
   (2) Are big and expensive houses easy to sell?
   (3) Are the desserts that the teacher taught us (to make) today difficult to make?

課　室　活　動　**Classroom Activities**

I. What 小美 Has Planned

Goal: Learning to talk about sequences of events.

Task: Read 小美 Xiaomei's schedule for June 6 and answer the following questions.

小美的記事本 (Xiaomei's Notes)

June 6 星期五	Notes
8:00 am	跟媽媽到學校付學費
9:00-12:00	上中文課
12:00	到李伯母家吃中飯
2:00-3:00	學書法
3:10-4:00	聽巴哈（Bāhā, Bach）音樂
5:00	跟朋友去看電影
8:00 pm	買包子

Write "T" or "F" (True or False) next to the statements below based on the information given above.

小美她 6 月 6 日…

1 （　）先去學校，再去吃飯。

2 （　）先吃中飯，再上中文課。

3 （　）先買包子，再去看電影。

4 （　）先上中文課，再學書法。

5 （　）先去李伯母家，再去看電影。

II. A Day in 大朋 Dapeng's Life

Goal: Learning to discuss things that your friends have done.

Task 1: Pair up with somebody. Take turns asking and answering questions about what 大朋 did yesterday.

在哪裡 / 買

怎麼來（去）

什麼時候

1 大朋的咖啡是在那家便利商店買的。

2

3

跟（誰）　　　　　　　誰

4

5

Task 2: Bring pictures to class. Use the pattern 是…的 to describe what is shown in the photos to the class. For example, "這張照片是在…照的／是今年三月照的／是跟朋友一起照的／…是怎麼去的／是…幫我們照的".

III. What Are Your Study Plans?

Goal: Learning to describe study plans and future plans.

Task: Tell the class of your plans, including how long you have been in Taiwan, how long you plan to stay, future study plans (in Taiwan or back in your country), and your future career plans.

IV. Have You Ever Worked?

Goal: Learning to describe your experience.

Task: If you have any work experience, please share it with the class. Other students are asked to pose questions when you are done.

文化 Bits of Chinese Culture

Addressing People in the Workplace

Being polite at all times is viewed as important by the Chinese. The workplace is no exceptions. How people are addressed depends on many factors.

The most common way to address a person is by their job title. For example, a manager can be addressed as 王經理 *Wáng Jīnglǐ* "Manager Wang" or a professor as 李教授 *Lǐ Jiàoshòu* "Professor Li." People are also addressed by titles that indicate the highest level of education they recieved. For example, a person with a Ph.D. can be addressed as 陳博士 *Chén Bóshì* "Dr. Chen" or as 文學博士陳月文 *Wénxué Bóshì Chén Yuè-wén* "Dr. of Literature Chen Yue-wen." Another method of address is based on profession, such as 張老師 *Zhāng Lǎoshī* "Teacher Zhang", or 王議員 *Wáng Yìyuán* "MP Wang" (MP = member of parliament). When one is unsure of someone's job title or profession, Miss 小姐 , Madam 女士 , or Mister 先生 is also polite.

▲ Addressing people by their job titles

Privacy Means Something Different for Taiwanese

Sometimes Taiwanese ask friends from abroad questions like "Where do you work?", "How much do you make?", "Are you married?", "How many children do you have?", and "Are they boys or girls?" While many foreigners consider these kinds of questions intrusive, in Taiwanese culture they are considered a sign of interest and a way of breaking the ice.

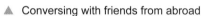
▲ Conversing with friends from abroad

Self-Assessment Checklist

I can discuss study plans and future plans.

20%   40%   60%   80%   100%

I can talk about sequences of events.

20%   40%   60%   80%   100%

I can describe past actions and experience.

20%   40%   60%   80%   100%

第十三課

生日快樂
Happy Birthday

Topic: 社交生活 **Social Life**

- Learning to make appointments on the phone.

- Learning to ask friends about their dietary preferences.

- Learning to compare cultures.

- Learning to express wishes to others on special occasions and to respond appropriately when others offer you wishes on special occasions.

生日快樂

Happy Birthday

對話一 Dialogue 1 13-01 13-A

怡 君	：喂，安同嗎？
安 同	：是，我就是。怡君，好久不見，聽說妳去花蓮？
怡 君	：我沒去花蓮，我剛從臺東回來。
安 同	：找我有什麼事？
怡 君	：明天是你的生日，對不對？
安 同	：啊，我怎麼忘了！最近太忙了，謝謝妳還記得。
怡 君	：當然記得！語言交換的時候，你那麼熱心教我西班牙文。
安 同	：不必客氣，妳也一樣。
怡 君	：明天我想請你吃晚飯，給你過生日。

安 同 ：妳太客氣了！我們在哪裡見面呢？

怡 君 ：明天我一下課，就去你們學校找你。

安 同 ：大概幾點？

怡 君 ：五點左右。

安 同 ：好，我會在學校門口等妳。

課文拼音 Text in Pinyin

Yíjūn	: Wéi, Āntóng ma?
Āntóng	: Shì, wǒ jiù shì. Yíjūn, hǎojiǔ bújiàn, tīngshuō nǐ qù Huālián?
Yíjūn	: Wǒ méi qù Huālián, wǒ gāng cóng Táidōng huílái.
Āntóng	: Zhǎo wǒ yǒu shénme shì?
Yíjūn	: Míngtiān shì nǐ de shēngrì, duì bú duì?
Āntóng	: A, wǒ zěnme wàngle! Zuìjìn tài máng le, xièxie nǐ hái jìde.
Yíjūn	: Dāngrán jìde! Yǔyán jiāohuàn de shíhòu, nǐ nàme rèxīn jiāo wǒ Xībānyá wén.
Āntóng	: Búbì kèqì, nǐ yě yíyàng.
Yíjūn	: Míngtiān wǒ xiǎng qǐng nǐ chī wǎnfàn, gěi nǐ guò shēngrì.
Āntóng	: Nǐ tài kèqì le! Wǒmen zài nǎlǐ jiànmiàn ne?
Yíjūn	: Míngtiān wǒ yí xiàkè, jiù qù nǐmen xuéxiào zhǎo nǐ.
Āntóng	: Dàgài jǐdiǎn?
Yíjūn	: Wǔdiǎn zuǒyòu.
Āntóng	: Hǎo, wǒ huì zài xuéxiào ménkǒu děng nǐ.

課文英譯 Text in English

Yijun	: Hello? Is this Antong?
Antong	: Yes, this is he. Yijun, long time no see. I heard you went to Hualien.
Yijun	: I didn't go to Hualien. I just got back from Taitung.
Antong	: Did you call me for some reason?
Yijun	: Tomorrow is your birthday, isn't it?
Antong	: Huh!? How did I forget!? I've been so busy lately. Thanks for remembering.
Yijun	: Of course I remember. When we were exchanging languages, you were so enthusiastic about teaching me Spanish.
Antong	: You are too kind. You were, too.
Yijun	: I would like to treat you to dinner tomorrow to celebrate your birthday.
Antong	: That is very kind of you. Where should we meet?
Yijun	: As soon as I'm out of class tomorrow, I will go to your school.
Antong	: About what time?
Yijun	: About five.
Antong	: Good. I will wait for you at the front gate of the school.

生詞一 Vocabulary   13-02

Vocabulary

1	生日	shēngrì	ㄕㄥ ㄖˋ	(N)	birthday
2	快樂	kuàilè	ㄎㄨㄞˋ ㄌㄜˋ	(Vs)	happy
3	回來	huílái	ㄏㄨㄟˊ ㄌㄞˊ	(Vi)	to come back
4	啊	a	ㄚˋ	(Ptc)	a particle indicating a realization
5	怎麼	zěnme	ㄗㄣˇ ㄇㄜˊ	(Adv)	How come?
6	忘（了）	wàngle	ㄨㄤˋ ㄌㄜˊ	(Vpt)	to forget
7	記得	jìde	ㄐㄧˋ ㄉㄜˊ	(Vst)	to remember
8	當然	dāngrán	ㄉㄤ ㄖㄢˊ	(Adv)	certainly, of course
9	語言	yǔyán	ㄩˇ ㄧㄢˊ	(N)	language

10	交換	jiāohuàn	ㄐㄧㄠ ㄏㄨㄢˋ	(V)	to exchange
11	那麼	nàme	ㄋㄚˋ ˙ㄇㄜ	(Adv)	so (very)
12	熱心	rèxīn	ㄖㄜˋ ㄒㄧㄣ	(Vs)	with enthusiasm
13	西班牙文	Xībānyá wén	ㄒㄧ ㄅㄢ ㄧㄚˊ ㄨㄣˊ	(N)	the Spanish language
14	一樣	yíyàng	ㄧˊ ㄧㄤˋ	(Vs)	the same, alike
15	過	guò	ㄍㄨㄛˋ	(V)	to celebrate
16	左右	zuǒyòu	ㄗㄨㄛˇ ㄧㄡˋ	(N)	approximately
17	門口	ménkǒu	ㄇㄣˊ ㄎㄡˇ	(N)	gate, entrance

Names

18	西班牙	Xībānyá	ㄒㄧ ㄅㄢ ㄧㄚˊ		Spain

Phrases

19	生日快樂	shēngrì kuàilè	ㄕㄥ ㄖˋ ㄎㄨㄞˋ ㄌㄜˋ		Happy Birthday.
20	我就是	wǒ jiù shì	ㄨㄛˇ ㄐㄧㄡˋ ㄕˋ		(said of self on the phone) This is s/he speaking.
21	好久不見	hǎojiǔ bújiàn	ㄏㄠˇ ㄐㄧㄡˇ ㄅㄨˊ ㄐㄧㄢˋ		long time no see
22	不必客氣	búbì kèqì	ㄅㄨˊ ㄅㄧˋ ㄎㄜˋ ㄑㄧˋ		No need to stand on formalities, i.e., It's my pleasure.
23	太客氣	tài kèqì	ㄊㄞˋ ㄎㄜˋ ㄑㄧˋ		That's very kind of you.

對話二 Dialogue 2 13-03 13-B

安	同	：怡君，謝謝妳請我到這麼有名的餐廳吃飯。
怡	君	：哪裡，哪裡！這是我給你的禮物。
安	同	：謝謝！真開心，今年有臺灣朋友給我過生日。
怡	君	：你想吃什麼？有沒有不吃的東西？
安	同	：我什麼都吃。
怡	君	：我已經訂了豬腳麵線和蛋。等一下你多吃一點。
安	同	：臺灣人過生日是不是都吃這些東西？
怡	君	：對啊！這是傳統，不過，現在大部分年輕人 過生日不吃這些東西了。
安	同	：那麼，你們過生日吃什麼呢？

怡　君：跟你們一樣，吃蛋糕。今天我也訂了一個生日蛋糕。

安　同：妳對我真好。

怡　君：安同，祝你生日快樂、萬事如意、心想事成。

安　同：謝謝！謝謝！

課文拼音 Text in Pinyin

Āntóng　　: Yíjūn, xièxie nǐ qǐng wǒ dào zhème yǒumíng de cāntīng chīfàn.

Yíjūn　　　: Nǎlǐ, nǎlǐ! Zhè shì wǒ gěi nǐ de lǐwù.

Āntóng　　: Xièxie! Zhēn kāixīn, jīnnián yǒu Táiwān péngyǒu gěi wǒ guò shēngrì.

Yíjūn　　　: Nǐ xiǎng chī shénme? Yǒu méi yǒu bù chī de dōngxi?

Āntóng　　: Wǒ shénme dōu chī.

Yíjūn　　　: Wǒ yǐjīng dìngle zhūjiǎo miànxiàn hàn dàn. Děng yíxià nǐ duō chī yìdiǎn.

Āntóng　　: Táiwān rén guò shēngrì shìbúshì dōu chī zhè xiē dōngxi?

Yíjūn　　　: Duì a! Zhè shì chuántǒng, búguò, xiànzài dà bùfèn niánqīng rén guò shēngrì bù chī zhè xiē dōngxi le.

Āntóng　　: Nàme, nǐmen guò shēngrì chī shénme ne?

Yíjūn　　　: Gēn nǐmen yíyàng, chī dàngāo. Jīntiān wǒ yě dìngle yí ge shēngrì dàngāo.

Āntóng　　: Nǐ duì wǒ zhēn hǎo.

Yíjūn　　　: Āntóng, zhù nǐ shēngrì kuàilè, wànshì rúyì, xīnxiǎng shìchéng.

Āntóng　　: Xièxie! Xièxie!

課文英譯 Text in English

Antong	: Yijun, thank you for asking me to eat at this well-known restaurant.
Yijun	: Not at all. Not at all. This is my gift to you.
Antong	: Thank you. I am really happy that a Taiwanese friend is celebrating my birthday with me this year.
Yijun	: What would you like to eat? Is there anything you don't eat?
Antong	: I eat anything.
Yijun	: I made a special order of pork knuckles with extra fine noodles and eggs before coming to the restaurant. (When it gets here,) dig in.
Antong	: Is that what Taiwanese eat on their birthdays?
Yijun	: Yes. This is a tradition, but most young people don't eat these things on their birthdays anymore.
Antong	: Then, what do you eat on your birthdays?
Yijun	: We eat cakes just like you. I also ordered a birthday cake.
Antong	: You are really nice to me.
Yijun	: Happy Birthday, Antong. I wish you the best in everything and may all your wishes come true.
Antong	: Thank you! Thank you!

生詞二 Vocabulary 2 13-04

Vocabulary

1	禮物	lǐwù	ㄌㄧˇ ㄨˋ	(N)	gift, present
2	今年	jīnnián	ㄐㄧㄣ ㄋㄧㄢˊ	(N)	this year
3	訂	dìng	ㄉㄧㄥˋ	(V)	to order (something in advance)
4	了	le	ㄌㄜ	(Ptc)	verbal particle indicating a completed action
5	豬腳	zhūjiǎo	ㄓㄨ ㄐㄧㄠˇ	(N)	pork knuckles
6	麵線	miànxiàn	ㄇㄧㄢˋ ㄒㄧㄢˋ	(N)	extra fine noodles
7	蛋	dàn	ㄉㄢˋ	(N)	egg

8	一點	yìdiǎn	ㄧ ㄉㄧㄢˇ	(Vs)	a little, some
9	傳統	chuántǒng	ㄔㄨㄢˊ ㄊㄨㄥˇ	(N)	tradition, customs
10	年輕	niánqīng	ㄋㄧㄢˊ ㄑㄧㄥ	(Vs)	young
11	蛋糕	dàngāo	ㄉㄢˋ ㄍㄠ	(N)	cake
12	對	duì	ㄉㄨㄟˋ	(Prep)	to
13	祝	zhù	ㄓㄨˋ	(V)	to wish (somebody happiness, good luck, etc.)

Phrases

14	哪裡，哪裡	Nǎlǐ, nǎlǐ	ㄋㄚˇ ㄌㄧˇ，ㄋㄚˇ ㄌㄧˇ	Don't mention it. It's my pleasure.
15	大部分	dà bùfèn	ㄉㄚˋ ㄅㄨˋ ㄈㄣ	most (of), mostly
16	萬事如意	wànshì rúyì	ㄨㄢˋ ㄕˋ ㄖㄨˊ ㄧˋ	May everything go your way.
17	心想事成	xīnxiǎng shìchéng	ㄒㄧㄣ ㄒㄧㄤˇ ㄕˋ ㄔㄥˊ	May all your wishes come true.

 文法 Grammar

I. 一 yī…就 jiù… *...as soon as...* 🎧 13-05　　 拼音、英譯 p.67

Function: The pattern " 一 A 就 B" indicates a sequence of events with B taking place right after A.

1 我一下課，就回來。

2 他一回國，就找工作。

3 我妹妹一回去，就給媽媽打電話。

Structures: The two events can be in the affirmative or in the negative. Both 一 and 就 are adverbs, which come after the subject. Note that a repeated subject can be omitted as below.

1 我一下課，就去吃晚飯。

2 他打算等那裡一沒人，就去拍照。

3 老闆今天早上一到公司，就不開心。

Questions: The A-not-A form is not possible. Both 嗎 or 是不是 can be used to form questions.

① 他一下課，就去學校找你嗎？

② 我們今天是不是比賽一結束，就一起去 KTV 唱歌？

練習 Exercise

Complete the following dialogues using the 一…就… pattern.

① A：昨天晚上你做什麼？　　　B：＿＿＿＿＿＿＿＿＿＿。
（到家，上網）

② A：你已經收到房租了嗎？　　　B：＿＿＿＿＿＿＿＿＿＿。
（上班，收到）

③ A：你什麼時候來找我？　　　　B：＿＿＿＿＿＿＿＿＿＿。
（下課，去你學校）

④ A：明天開始放假，你要做什麼？　B：＿＿＿＿＿＿＿＿＿＿。

⑤ A：你明天下課以後，要做什麼？　B：＿＿＿＿＿＿＿＿＿＿。

II. Completed Action with Verbal 了 le  13-06　　　 拼音、英譯 p.67

Function: The verbal 了 *le* is added after the verb to indicate that an action or event has been completed or has taken place. Compare the following sentences.

我買了三張車票。　vs.　我要買三張車票。

1 我剛在便利商店喝了咖啡。   **2** 我昨天吃了很多東西。

3 今天早上我喝了一杯咖啡。   **4** 他租了一個漂亮的房子。

Structures:

 Negation:

The negation is marked by the negation marker 沒 *méi*. Note that the verbal 了 does not occur in negative sentences.

1 我今天沒吃午餐。

2 我最近很忙，一星期都沒看電視。

3 昨天跟朋友去過生日，所以我沒寫功課。

Questions: To ask a question, 沒有 *méi yǒu* is added at the end of the sentence.

1 弟弟吃了午餐沒有？

2 下個月的學費，他付了沒有？

3 今晚的籃球比賽開始了沒有？

Usage: The verbal 了 *le* does not appear in negative sentences.

Wrong: Correct:

*我沒吃了晚飯。   我沒吃晚飯。

練習 Exercise 13-07

Listen to the recording a couple of times and then put check marks next to the activities based on who did and didn't do them.

	安同		如玉		月美		田中	
	做了	沒做	做了	沒做	做了	沒做	做了	沒做

	安同		如玉		月美		田中	
	做了	沒做	做了	沒做	做了	沒做	做了	沒做

III. 不 Negation vs. 沒 Negation   🎧 13-08    拼音、英譯 p.68

Function: Both 不 *bù* and 沒 *méi* are negative markers, but they are used differently. Negation is best understood in terms of how a negative marker interacts with various verb types.

Verb Types ╲ Negator	不	沒（有）
Action Verb	✓	✓
State Verb	✓	✗
Process Verb	✗	✓

A. Negation of action verbs

1. 不 negation, there are two interpretations:

(1) Habitual

a. 我們星期六不上課。　　　　b. 學生常不吃早餐。

59

(2) Intention not to

    a. 我不去圖書館。   b. 他不找工作。

2. 沒 negation indicates a non-happening in the past.

(1) 昨天我沒打電話給他。

(2) 上個星期我沒跟同學去 KTV。

(3) 今天我沒坐捷運來上課。我坐公車。

B. Negation of state verbs

State verbs can only be negated by 不, which indicates the contrary.

(1) 今天不熱，我想出去逛逛。

(2) 他說中文不難學，可是中國字不好寫。

(3) 我不舒服，今天不想出去。

C. Negation of process verbs

Process verbs can only be negated by 沒 which indicates non-happening.

(1) 中文課還沒結束，所以我不能回國。

(2) 我沒忘。你先去學校，我等一下去找你。

(3) 我還沒決定要不要去旅行。

Usage: In Taiwan, 沒 negation is less common than 沒有 negation. E.g., 我沒有買手機。*Wǒ méi yǒu mǎi shǒujī.* "I didn't buy a cell phone". In mainland China, 我沒買手機。*Wǒ méi mǎi shǒujī.* "I didn't buy a cell phone" is more common.

練習 Exercise

Put 沒 or 不 in the blanks and explain briefly why you did.

	Sentences	Why
Example	我們下星期一（ 不 ）上課。	Negation of action verbs
1	他常常不來工作，也（　　）打電話給老闆。	

	Sentences	Why
2	我覺得今天（　　）熱。	
3	昨天我（　　）跟他去逛夜市。	
4	這家牛肉麵店（　　）便宜。	
5	比賽還（　　）開始，我先去買杯咖啡。	

IV. All-inclusive with Question Words 13-09

Function: Question words can appear in declarative sentences in Chinese. When they do, they often co-occur with 都 *dōu* "all" to indicate totality without exception, that is, total inclusion in affirmative sentences and total exclusion in negative sentences.

		Negative	Question
誰	everyone	nobody	who?
哪裡	everywhere	nowhere	where?
什麼	everything	nothing	what?
什麼時候	anytime, always	never	when?
怎麼 + V	whichever way	no way, never	how?

❶ 誰都喜歡去旅行。

❷ 哪裡都有好吃的東西。

❸ 他什麼都想買。

❹ 弟弟什麼時候都在上網。

❺ 他們學校很方便，怎麼去都能到。

Structures:

 Negation:

In negative sentences, question words are used with either 都 *dōu* or 也 *yě* to indicate total exclusion. The negation marker 不 *bù* or 沒 *méi* comes after 都 *dōu* / 也 *yě*.

1 誰也不喜歡難看的東西。

2 昨天我哪裡都沒去，在家看電視。

3 我今天什麼也不想吃。

4 下個星期，我什麼時候都不在家，我要去旅行。

5 中國菜很難做，我怎麼做都不好吃。

 Questions: This pattern goes with 嗎 *ma* only.

1 這家餐廳的東西什麼都好吃嗎？

2 你今天什麼時候都在公司嗎？

練習 Exercise

Rewrite the following sentences into all-inclusive or all-exclusive patterns.

Example 大家都喜歡我。 → 誰都喜歡我。

1 每一個人都很忙。→＿＿＿＿＿＿＿＿＿＿＿＿＿＿＿＿＿。

2 李先生有錢、有房子、有車子…。→＿＿＿＿＿＿＿＿＿＿。

3 他早上、中午、晚上都在上網。→＿＿＿＿＿＿＿＿＿＿。

4 這裡有中國餐廳，那裡也有中國餐廳。→＿＿＿＿＿＿＿。

5 這種包子，熱的好吃，冷的也好吃。→＿＿＿＿＿＿＿。

V. More/Less...Than Planned with 多 duō / 少 shǎo ＋ Verb…

 拼音、英譯 p.70

🎧 13-10

Function: Pre-verbal 多 *duō* "more" or 少 *shǎo* "less" indicates "more" or "less/fewer" than planned.

❶ 我最近沒錢了，應該少買東西。

❷ 我中文不好，應該多看書，少看電視。

❸ 我們明天應該多穿衣服嗎？

Usage: 一點 *yìdiǎn* "a little bit" is often used to modify the object. This pattern can refer to events in the past or in the future.

❶ 他喜歡臺灣，想多學一點中文。

❷ 昨天我朋友來我家，我多做了一點菜。

❸ 她今天太累了，想少做一點功課。

練習 Exercise

Refer to the pictures below and offer him/her suggestions.

❶

她應該 ＿＿＿＿＿＿＿＿＿＿＿。

❷

他應該 ＿＿＿＿＿＿＿＿＿＿＿。

❸

他應該 ＿＿＿＿＿＿＿＿＿＿＿。

❹

她應該 ＿＿＿＿＿＿＿＿。（甜點）

VI. 是不是 shìbúshì *is it true?* 13-11

Function: This pattern seeks confirmation for information already known or obvious from the context.

❶ 你是不是在家等我？　　❷ 那家餐廳是不是很有名？
❸ 你是不是剛旅行回來？

Structures: Subject ＋是不是＋VP？

Usage:

1. 是不是 questions are quite different from 嗎 questions and A-not-A questions. It is not asking for new information but is asking for confirmation of old information. Please look at the differences below.

   (1) 你銀行有錢嗎？　　　　(2) 你銀行有沒有錢？
   (3) 你銀行是不是有錢？

2. In the following sentences, A-not-A cannot be used. 是不是 shìbúshì or 嗎 ma can be used.

   (1) 你比他高：*你比不比他高？　　*你比他高不高？
   　　　　　　　你是不是比他高？
   (2) 你最近太忙了：*你最近太忙不忙？
   　　　　　　　你是不是最近太忙了？

練習 Exercise

Please insert 是不是 into the appropriate place in the sentences.

Example　他已經訂了豬腳麵線。 → <u>他是不是已經訂了豬腳麵線？</u>

❶ 我們明天給他過生日。→ _____ ？
❷ 你的學費公司替你付。→ _____ ？
❸ 他來臺灣學中文。　 → _____ ？
❹ 你打算明年回國。　 → _____ ？
❺ 他很喜歡逛夜市。　 → _____ ？

VII. Comparison with 跟 gēn…一樣 yíyàng 13-12

拼音、英譯 p.71

Function: This pattern is used to compare two people or things and indicate whether they are the same (equal) or not the same. The similar/same quality of the persons or things being compared, if any, follow 一樣.

❶ 這支手機跟那支手機一樣。

❷ 我的生日跟她的生日一樣，都是八月十七日。

❸ 他跟我一樣，都常游泳。

Structures: A 跟 B 一樣 (State VP).

❶ 你點的菜跟我點的一樣。

❷ 我跟我妹妹一樣高。

❸ 姐姐租的房子跟我租的一樣貴。

❹ 我跟我朋友一樣喜歡看電視。

Negation:

1. The negation 不 *bù* precedes 一樣 *yíyàng* to indicate that the two nouns are different in quality.

   (1) 中國茶跟日本茶不一樣。

   (2) 我跟妹妹不一樣高。

2. The negation marker 不 *bù* can also precede 跟 *gēn*, but when it does, it negates the object to be compared with, i.e., the 跟 *gēn*... part, not the "same" part.

   他不跟我一樣高，跟小王一樣高。

Questions: To ask a question, the A-not-A pattern can be used with 一樣 *yíyàng* or 是不是 *shìbúshì* can be placed in front of 一樣.

❶ 小籠包跟包子一樣不一樣？

❷ 小籠包跟包子是不是一樣？

❸ 今年的生意是不是跟去年的一樣好？

❹ 說中文跟寫中文是不是一樣難？

練習 Exercise

Match the activities to the pictures on the chart below, then write sentences using the …跟…一樣….

好吃：	難學：	好喝：
喜歡…：	貴：	

1 我

2 我做的牛肉麵

3 20000 元 / 我的手機 20000 元

4 茶

5 語言 / 中文

6 20000 元 / 她的手機 20000 元

7 我弟弟

8 媽媽做的牛肉麵

9 咖啡

10 ハウス / 日文

語法例句拼音與英譯
Grammar Examples in Pinyin and English

I. 一 yī··· 就 jiù··· *as soon as...*

Function:

1. Wǒ yí xiàkè, jiù huílái.
2. Tā yì huíguó, jiù zhǎo gōngzuò.
3. Wǒ mèimei yì huíqù, jiù gěi māma dǎ diànhuà.

Function:

1. I will return as soon as class is over.
2. He looked for a job as soon as he returned to his country.
3. My sister called Mom right after she got home.

Structures:

1. Wǒ yí xiàkè, jiù qù chī wǎnfàn.
2. Tā dǎsuàn děng nàlǐ yì méi rén, jiù qù pāizhào.
3. Lǎobǎn jīntiān zǎoshàng yí dào gōngsī, jiù bù kāixīn.

Structures:

1. As soon as I get out of class, I'll go eat dinner.
2. He plans to go take pictures as soon as there is nobody there.
3. The boss was upset as soon as he arrived at the office this morning.

Questions:

1. Tā yí xiàkè, jiù qù xuéxiào zhǎo nǐ ma?
2. Wǒmen jīntiān shìbúshì bǐsài yì jiéshù, jiù yìqǐ qù KTV chànggē?

Questions:

1. Did he go to school to see you right after he got out of class?
2. Are we going to KTV today together right after the game is over?

II. Completed Action with Verbal 了 le

Function:

Wǒ mǎile sān zhāng chēpiào.
Wǒ yào mǎi sān zhāng chēpiào.

1. Wǒ gāng zài biànlì shāngdiàn hēle kāfēi.
2. Wǒ zuótiān chīle hěn duō dōngxi.
3. Jīntiān zǎoshàng wǒ hēle yì bēi kāfēi.
4. Tā zūle yí ge piàoliàng de fángzi.

Function:

I bought three tickets.
I am going to buy three tickets.

1. I just had coffe at a convenience store.
2. I ate a lot of stuff yesterday.
3. I drank a cup of coffee this morning.
4. He rented a beautiful house.

Structures:

✏️ **Negation:**

1. Wǒ jīntiān méi chī wǔcān.
2. Wǒ zuìjìn hěn máng, yì xīngqí dōu méi kàn diànshì.
3. Zuótiān gēn péngyǒu qù guò shēngrì, suǒyǐ wǒ méi xiě gōngkè.

✏️ **Questions:**

1. Dìdi chīle wǔcān méi yǒu?
2. Xià ge yuè de xuéfèi, tā fùle méi yǒu?
3. Jīnwǎn de lánqiú bǐsài kāishǐle méi yǒu?

Usage:

Correct:

Wǒ méi chī wǎnfàn.

Structures:

✏️ **Negation:**

1. I didn't eat lunch today.
2. I have been very busy lately. I have not watched TV for a week.
3. Yesterday, I went to celebrate my friend's birthday so I did not do the homework.

✏️ **Questions:**

1. Did little brother eat his lunch?
2. Did he pay the tuition for next month?
3. Has tonight's basketball game started yet?

Usage:

Correct:

I didn't have dinner.

III. 不 Negation vs. 沒 Negation

Function:

A. Negation of action verbs

1. (1) Habitual
   a. Wǒmen xīngqíliù bú shàngkè.
   b. Xuéshēng cháng bù chī zǎocān.

   (2) Intention not to
   a. Wǒ bú qù túshūguǎn.
   b. Tā bù zhǎo gōngzuò.

2. (1) Zuótiān wǒ méi dǎ diànhuà gěi tā.
   (2) Shàng ge xīngqí wǒ méi gēn tóngxué qù KTV.
   (3) Jīntiān wǒ méi zuò jiéyùn lái shàngkè. Wǒ zuò gōngchē.

Function:

A. Negation of action verbs

1. (1) Habitual
   a. We don't go to school on Saturdays.
   b. Students often don't eat breakfast.

   (2) Intention not to
   a. I'm not going to go to the library.
   b. He's not looking for a job.

2. (1) I didn't call him yesterday.
   (2) I didn't go to KTV with classmates last week.
   (3) I didn't come to class by MRT today. I took a bus.

B. Negation of state verbs

(1) Jīntiān bú rè, wǒ xiǎng chūqù guàngguàng.

(2) Tā shuō Zhōngwén bù nán xué, kěshì Zhōngguó zì bù hǎo xiě.

(3) Wǒ bù shūfú, jīntiān bù xiǎng chūqù.

C. Negation of process verbs

(1) Zhōngwén kè hái méi jiéshù, suǒyǐ wǒ bù néng huíguó.

(2) Wǒ méi wàng. Nǐ xiān qù xuéxiào, wǒ děng yíxià qù zhǎo nǐ.

(3) Wǒ hái méi juédìng yào bú yào qù lǚxíng?

B. Negation of state verbs

(1) It is not hot today. I'd like to go out and look around.

(2) He said Chinese is not difficult to learn, but Chinese characters are hard to write.

(3) I don't feel well. I don't want to go out today.

C. Negation of process verbs

(1) My Chinese classes have not ended yet, so I can't go back to my country.

(2) I didn't forget. You go to school first and I will go see you later.

(3) I still have not decided whether to take a trip or not.

IV. All-inclusive with Question Words

Function:

❶ Shéi dōu xǐhuān qù lǚxíng.
❷ Nǎlǐ dōu yǒu hǎochī de dōngxi.
❸ Tā shénme dōu xiǎng mǎi.
❹ Dìdi shénme shíhòu dōu zài shàngwǎng.
❺ Tāmen xuéxiào hěn fāngbiàn, zěnme qù dōu néng dào.

Function:

❶ Everyone likes to travel.
❷ There's delicious food everywhere you go.
❸ He wants to buy everything.
❹ My younger brother is online all the time.
❺ Their school is conveniently located. You can use any way (means of transportation) to get there.

Structures:

🖋 **Negation:**

❶ Shéi yě bù xǐhuān nánkàn de dōngxi.
❷ Zuótiān wǒ nǎlǐ dōu méi qù, zài jiā kàn diànshì.
❸ Wǒ jīntiān shénme yě bù xiǎng chī.
❹ Xià ge xīngqí, wǒ shénme shíhòu dōu bú zài jiā, wǒ yào qù lǚxíng.
❺ Zhōngguó cài hěn nán zuò, wǒ zěnme zuò dōu bù hǎochī.

Structures:

🖋 **Negation:**

❶ No one likes ugly things.
❷ I didn't go anywhere yesterday. I watched TV at home.
❸ I don't feel like eating anything today.
❹ Next week, I won't be home the whole time. I will be traveling.
❺ Chinese food is hard to make. No matter what I do, it tastes bad.

✎ Questions:

1 Zhè jiā cāntīng de dōngxi shénme dōu hǎochī ma?

2 Nǐ jīntiān shénme shíhòu dōu zài gōngsī ma?

✎ Questions:

1 Is everything in this restaurant tasty?

2 Will you be at the office all day today?

V. More/Less...Than Planned with 多 duō / 少 shǎo ＋ Verb…

Function:

1 Wǒ zuìjìn méi qián le, yīnggāi shǎo mǎi dōngxi.

2 Wǒ Zhōngwén bù hǎo, yīnggāi duō kànshū, shǎo kàn diànshì.

3 Wǒmen míngtiān yīnggāi duō chuān yīfú ma?

Function:

1 I haven't had any money recently, so I should spend less (than usual).

2 My Chinese is not good. I should study more and watch TV less.

3 Should we wear more clothes than usual tomorrow?

Usage:

1 Tā xǐhuān Táiwān, xiǎng duō xué yìdiǎn Zhōngwén.

2 Zuótiān wǒ péngyǒu lái wǒ jiā, wǒ duō zuòle yìdiǎn cài.

3 Tā jīntiān tài lèi le, xiǎng shǎo zuò yìdiǎn gōngkè.

Usage:

1 He likes Taiwan and wants to study Chinese a bit more.

2 Friends of mine came to my house yesterday. I made a little extra food.

3 She is too tired today and wants to do less homework (than her teacher assigned.)

VI. 是不是 shìbúshì *is it true?*

Function:

1 Nǐ shìbúshì zài jiā děng wǒ?

2 Nà jiā cāntīng shìbúshì hěn yǒumíng?

3 Nǐ shìbúshì gāng lǚxíng huílái?

Function:

1 You are waiting for me at home, right?

2 That restaurant is well-known, right?

3 You just come back from a trip, right?

Usage:

1. (1) Nǐ yínháng yǒu qián ma?

   (2) Nǐ yínháng yǒu méi yǒu qián?

   (3) Nǐ yínháng shìbúshì yǒu qián?

Usage:

1. (1) (We're having problems. We need some money.) Do you have some money in the bank?

   (2) (same as above)

   (3) (We are having problems. We need some money.) You have some money in the bank, right?

2. (1) Nǐ bǐ tā gāo.

Nǐ shìbúshì bǐ tā gāo?

(2) Nǐ zuìjìn tài máng le.

Nǐ shìbúshì zuìjìn tài máng le?

2. (1) You are taller than him.

You are taller than him, right?

(2) You've been too busy lately.

You have been too busy lately, right?

VII. Comparison with 跟 gēn…一樣 yíyàng

Function:

❶ Zhè zhī shǒujī gēn nà zhī shǒujī yíyàng.

❷ Wǒ de shēngrì gēn tā de shēngrì yíyàng, dōu shì bāyuè shíqī rì.

❸ Tā gēn wǒ yíyàng, dōu cháng yóuyǒng.

Function:

❶ This cellphone is exactly the same as that one.

❷ My birthday is the same as hers. They're both on August 17th.

❸ He and I are the same. We both swim often. (We are alike.)

Structures:

❶ Nǐ diǎn de cài gēn wǒ diǎn de yíyàng.

❷ Wǒ gēn wǒ mèimei yíyàng gāo.

❸ Jiějie zū de fángzi gēn wǒ zū de yíyàng guì.

❹ Wǒ gēn wǒ péngyǒu yíyàng xǐhuān kàn diànshì.

Structures:

❶ We both ordered the same dish.

❷ I am as tall as my younger sister.

❸ The house that my older sister rents is as expensive as the one I rent.

❹ My friend and I are the same. We both enjoy watching TV.

✏ Negation:

1. (1) Zhōngguó chá gēn Rìběn chá bù yíyàng.

(2) Wǒ gēn mèimei bù yíyàng gāo.

2. Tā bù gēn wǒ yíyàng gāo, gēn Xiǎo Wáng yíyàng gāo.

✏ Negation:

1. (1) Chinese tea and Japanese tea are different.

(2) My younger sister and I are not the same height.

2. He and I are not the same height. He and Xiao Wang are the same height.

✏ Questions:

❶ Xiǎolóngbāo gēn bāozi yíyàng bù yíyàng?

❷ Xiǎolóngbāo gēn bāozi shì bú shì yíyàng?

❸ Jīnnián de shēngyì shì bú shì gēn qùnián de yíyàng hǎo?

❹ Shuō Zhōngwén gēn xiě Zhōngwén shì bú shì yíyàng nán?

✏ Questions:

❶ Is a xiaolongbao the same as a baozi?

❷ Are xiaolongbao the same as baozi?

❸ Is business this year as good as it was last year?

❹ Is speaking Chinese as difficult as writing Chinese?

課 室 活 動 **Classroom Activities**

I. Going to Night Markets

Goal: Learning to ask people about their preferences.

Task: You found out that your classmate went to the night market last night. You want to know if he did any of the following.

A：你昨天逛夜市，吃了臭豆腐沒有？

B：(i) 沒有，我點了小籠包。

　　(ii) 吃了，我吃了臭豆腐

　　(iii) 我沒吃臭豆腐。

II. How Do You Celebrate Your Birthday?

Goal: Learning to compare briefly different cultures.

Task: Pair up with someone and ask each other how birthdays are celebrated in each other's home country. Check each item that applies. When you are done, consolidate the answers with everyone in class and have a representative report the similarities and differences in the ways birthdays are celebrated in different countries.

怎麼過生日？ 　　　　國名	美國 USA									
家人給你過生日										
朋友給你過生日										
在家裡過										
在外面（餐廳）吃飯										
吃蛋糕										
朋友給你禮物										
自己買蛋糕請朋友吃										
吃豬腳麵線										
跟我們國家不一樣										

III. Calling a Friend

Goal: Learning to make appointments over the phone.

Task: Your teacher's birthday is tomorrow. Call your classmate and talk about inviting the teacher out for a meal. (Pair up with the person next to you. In your conversation, please ask: Why ask him/her to a meal? When should you go? Where should you go? How will everybody meet up?)

IV. Congratulatory Words

Goal: Learning to convey wishes on happy occasions.

Task: Today is your teacher's birthday. Write a card to your teacher.

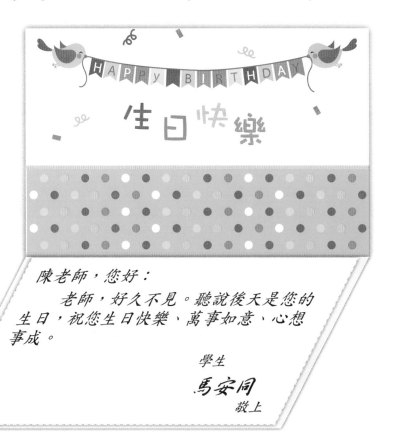

陳老師，您好：

　　老師，好久不見。聽說後天是您的生日，祝您生日快樂、萬事如意、心想事成。

學生

馬安同

敬上

文化 *Bits of Chinese Culture*

Congratulatory Expressions in Chinese

Congratulatory expressions are used to congratulate people on special occasions. Chinese people value this in interpersonal relationships and like to express caring thoughts at the right place, at the right time, and for the right occasion. Most of these sayings are four-character expressions with fixed and auspicious meanings. The most all-purpose congratulatory expression is probably 萬事如意、心想事成 *wànshì rúyì, xīnxiǎng shìchéng* "I wish you all the best and that all your wishes come true."

▲ 蕙風堂／提供

▲ Common congratulatory expressions

Taiwanese Birthdays

Traditionally, Chinese people celebrate their birthdays based on the lunar calendar, but today, most people celebrate their

▲ 抓週 tradition for babies at their first year of age

birthdays as indicated the Gregorian calendar. Birthdays are very important to the Taiwanese. Celebrations for infants are held when they are one-month and one-year old. Major decades, such as 60, 70, and 80-years of age, are of particular importance. The ancient tradition of 抓週 *zhuāzhōu* (grabbing at the first year) is still practiced. For this custom, a child is surrounded by a number of items on his first birthday. The item that he grabs is said to indicate what kind of character he will have and his future profession.

▲ Big birthday celebrations for major decades

Self-Assessment Checklist

I can make appointments on the phone.

| 20% | 40% | 60% | 80% | 100% |

I can ask friends about their dietary preferences.

| 20% | 40% | 60% | 80% | 100% |

I can compare cultures.

| 20% | 40% | 60% | 80% | 100% |

I can express wishes to others on special occasions and can respond appropriately when others offer me wishes on special occasions.

| 20% | 40% | 60% | 80% | 100% |

LESSON 14

第十四課

天氣這麼冷！
It's So Cold!

學習目標 Learning Objectives

Topic: 天氣 The Weather

· Learning to talk about weather conditions, including typhoons.

· Learning to talk about the four seasons and explain why you like or dislike them.

· Learning to compare events.

· Learning to make simple statements about experiences, e.g., trips.

天氣這麼冷！

It's So Cold!

對話一 Dialogue 1   14-01 14-A

如 玉	：	外面風那麼大，我覺得今天比昨天冷。 臺灣會不會下雪？
明 華	：	很高的山會下雪。玉山常下雪。 美國呢？開始下雪了吧？
如 玉	：	還沒有。每年差不多十二月開始。 下雪的時候，我常去山上滑雪。
明 華	：	我怕冷。我比較喜歡春天。
如 玉	：	春天不錯，天氣很舒服。
明 華	：	我去年五月在紐約玩了兩個星期。那個時候， 天氣很好，風景也很漂亮，我玩得非常開心。
如 玉	：	我在臺灣住了半年多了。有一點想家。
明 華	：	新年快到了。想回去看父母嗎？

如	玉	：我打算十二月底回去。想跟我去美國玩嗎？
明	華	：冬天太冷了。不過，我想明年秋天去看紅葉。 對了，妳什麼時候回來？
如	玉	：因為我們只放十天的假，所以一月五號回來。

課文拼音 Text in Pinyin

Rúyù : Wàimiàn fēng nàme dà, wǒ juéde jīntiān bǐ zuótiān lěng.
Táiwān huì bú huì xiàxuě?

Mínghuá : Hěn gāo de shān huì xiàxuě. Yùshān cháng xiàxuě. Měiguó ne?
Kāishǐ xiàxuě le ba?

Rúyù : Hái méi yǒu. Měi nián chābùduō shí'èryuè kāishǐ. Xiàxuě de shíhòu,
wǒ cháng qù shānshàng huáxuě.

Mínghuá : Wǒ pà lěng. Wǒ bǐjiào xǐhuān chūntiān.

Rúyù : Chūntiān búcuò, tiānqì hěn shūfú.

Mínghuá : Wǒ qùnián wǔyuè zài Niǔyuē wánle liǎng ge xīngqí. Nà ge shíhòu, tiānqì hěn
hǎo, fēngjǐng yě hěn piàoliàng, wǒ wán de fēicháng kāixīn.

Rúyù : Wǒ zài Táiwān zhùle bàn nián duō le. Yǒu yìdiǎn xiǎng jiā.

Mínghuá : Xīnnián kuài dào le. Xiǎng huíqù kàn fùmǔ ma?

Rúyù : Wǒ dǎsuàn shí'èryuè dǐ huíqù. Xiǎng gēn wǒ qù Měiguó wán ma?

Mínghuá : Dōngtiān tài lěng le. Búguò, wǒ xiǎng míngnián qiūtiān qù kàn hóngyè.
Duìle, nǐ shénme shíhòu huílái?

Rúyù : Yīnwèi wǒmen zhǐ fàng shí tiān de jià, suǒyǐ yīyuè wǔhào huílái.

課文英譯 Text in English

Ruyu	: It is windy outside. I think it's colder today than yesterday. Does it snow in Taiwan?

Ruyu : It is windy outside. I think it's colder today than yesterday.
Does it snow in Taiwan?

Minghua : It snows on high mountains. It snows on Yushan frequently. And the US?
It has probably started snowing (there).

Ruyu : Not yet. Every year around December, it starts. When it snows, I often go skiing in the mountains.

Minghua : I don't like the cold. I like spring better.

Ruyu : Spring isn't bad. The weather is nice.

Minghua : Last May, I was in New York having a good time for two weeks.
The weather was very nice then and the scenery was beautiful. I had a great time.

Ruyu : I have lived in Taiwan for over half a year now. I'm a little homesick.

Minghua : It is almost New Year's. Are you thinking about going back to see your parents?

Ruyu : I plan to go back at the end of December. Would you like to go with me to the US?

Minghua : The winter is too cold, but I would like to go see the autumn leaves next year.
By the way, when are you coming back?

Ruyu : We only have 10 days off, so I will be back January 5th.

生詞一 Vocabulary 1 14-02

Vocabulary

1	天氣	tiānqì	ㄊㄧㄢ ㄑㄧˋ	(N)	weather
2	冷	lěng	ㄌㄥˇ	(Vs)	cold
3	風	fēng	ㄈㄥ	(N)	wind
4	滑雪	huáxuě	ㄏㄨㄚˊ ㄒㄩㄝˇ	(V-sep)	to ski
5	春天	chūntiān	ㄔㄨㄣ ㄊㄧㄢ	(N)	spring (season)
6	想	xiǎng	ㄒㄧㄤˇ	(Vst)	to miss (someone)
7	新年	xīnnián	ㄒㄧㄣ ㄋㄧㄢˊ	(N)	New Year
8	快	kuài	ㄎㄨㄞˋ	(Adv)	soon
9	父母	fùmǔ	ㄈㄨˋ ㄇㄨˇ	(N)	parents

10	冬天	dōngtiān	ㄉㄨㄥ ㄊㄧㄢ	(N)	winter (season)
11	明年	míngnián	ㄇㄧㄥ ㄋㄧㄢ	(N)	next year
12	秋天	qiūtiān	ㄑㄧㄡ ㄊㄧㄢ	(N)	autumn (season)
13	紅葉	hóngyè	ㄏㄨㄥ ㄧㄝ	(N)	red maple leaves
14	只	zhǐ	ㄓ	(Adv)	only, merely

Names

| 15 | 玉山 | Yùshān | ㄩ ㄕㄢ | | Yu Shan (Mount Jade), tallest mountain in central Taiwan |
| 16 | 紐約 | Niǔyuē | ㄋㄧㄡ ㄩㄝ | | New York |

Phrases

| 17 | 下雪 | xiàxuě | ㄒㄧㄚ ㄒㄩㄝ | | to snow |
| 18 | 十二月底 | shí'èryuè dǐ | ㄕ ㄦ ㄩㄝ ㄉㄧ | | the end of December |

對話二 Dialogue 2 14-03 14-B

明　　華：如玉，雨下得這麼大，妳怎麼沒帶傘呢？

如　　玉：我昨天帶了，可是今天忘了帶。

明　　華：颱風快要來了。

如　　玉：我已經聽說了。

明　　華：這裡每年夏天都有颱風。颱風來的時候，風和雨都很大，做什麼都很不方便。

如　　玉：是啊！哪裡都濕濕的。真討厭。

明　　華：電視新聞說，這次的颱風會比上次的更大，請大家多小心。

如　　玉：希望這次的沒有上次的那麼可怕。

明　　華：如玉，妳看！雨停了。

如　　玉：太好了！謝謝你的傘，再見。

明　　華：不客氣。小心慢走。

課文拼音 Text in Pinyin

Mínghuá	: Rúyù, yǔ xià de zhème dà, nǐ zěnme méi dài sǎn ne?
Rúyù	: Wǒ zuótiān dài le, kěshì jīntiān wàngle dài.
Mínghuá	: Táifēng kuài yào lái le.
Rúyù	: Wǒ yǐjīng tīngshuō le.
Mínghuá	: Zhèlǐ měi nián xiàtiān dōu yǒu táifēng. Táifēng lái de shíhòu, fēng hàn yǔ dōu hěn dà, zuò shénme dōu hěn bù fāngbiàn.
Rúyù	: Shì a! Nǎlǐ dōu shīshī de. Zhēn tǎoyàn.
Mínghuá	: Diànshì xīnwén shuō, zhè cì de táifēng huì bǐ shàng cì de gèng dà, qǐng dàjiā duō xiǎoxīn.
Rúyù	: Xīwàng zhè cì de méi yǒu shàng cì de nàme kěpà.
Mínghuá	: Rúyù, nǐ kàn! Yǔ tíng le.
Rúyù	: Tài hǎo le! Xièxie nǐ de sǎn, zàijiàn.
Mínghuá	: Búkèqì. Xiǎoxīn màn zǒu.

課文英譯 Text in English

Minghua : Ruyu, as heavy as it's raining, why didn't you bring an umbrella?

Ruyu : I brought it yesterday, but I forgot to bring it today.

Minghua : A typhoon is coming.

Ruyu : Yes, I've heard.

Minghua : We have typhoons every summer. When typhoons hit, we get heavy wind and rain. It gets very inconvenient to do anything.

Ruyu : Yeah. It gets wet everywhere. I hate it.

Minghua : The TV news says this typhoon is bigger than the last one and advised everyone to be extra cautious.

Ruyu : I hope the one this time is not as scary as the last one.

Minghua : Ruyu, Look. The rain has stopped.

Ruyu : Great! Thank you for the umbrella. See you.

Minghua : You're welcome. Take care.

生詞二 Vocabulary 2 14-04

Vocabulary

1	雨	yǔ	ㄩˇ	(N)	rain
2	傘	sǎn	ㄙㄢˇ	(N)	umbrella
3	颱風	táifēng	ㄊㄞˊ ㄈㄥ	(N)	typhoon
4	要	yào	ㄧㄠˋ	(Vaux)	will, going to
5	夏天	xiàtiān	ㄒㄧㄚˋ ㄊㄧㄢ	(N)	summer (season)
6	濕	shī	ㄕ	(Vs)	wet
7	討厭	tǎoyàn	ㄊㄠˇ ㄧㄢˋ	(Vs)	annoying
8	新聞	xīnwén	ㄒㄧㄣ ㄨㄣˊ	(N)	news
9	更	gèng	ㄍㄥˋ	(Adv)	even (more, less, etc.)
10	大家	dàjiā	ㄉㄚˋ ㄐㄧㄚ	(N)	everyone
11	小心	xiǎoxīn	ㄒㄧㄠˇ ㄒㄧㄣ	(Vs)	to be careful, to take care
12	可怕	kěpà	ㄎㄜˇ ㄆㄚˋ	(Vs)	scary

| 13 | 停 | tíng | ㄊㄧㄥˊ | (Vp) | to stop |

Phrases

14	下雨	xiàyǔ	ㄒㄧㄚˋ ㄩˇ		to rain
15	這次	zhè cì	ㄓㄜˋ ㄘˋ		this time
16	上次	shàng cì	ㄕㄤˋ ㄘˋ		last time
17	慢走	màn zǒu	ㄇㄢˋ ㄗㄡˇ		Bye. Take care.

文法 Grammar

I. Time-Duration after verbal 了 le 🎧 14-05  拼音、英譯 p.90

Function: This pattern indicates the duration of a completed activity.

❶ 媽媽的朋友在臺北玩了三天。
❷ 老師在美國住了一年。
❸ 李小姐在語言中心工作了一個月。

Structures: The primary structure is verb+Time Duration.

1. If the verb is transitive and has an object after it, the verb must be repeated.

    (1) 他租房子租了半年。
    (2) 他住臺北住了三年。

2. No verb repetition is needed if the object is placed elsewhere.

    (1) 房子他只租了半年。
    (2) 臺北他只住了三年。

 Questions:

❶ 那間房子你租了一年半嗎？
❷ 你是不是在這裡等了一個鐘頭？
❸ 陳老闆去年是不是在紐約住了半年？

練習 Exercise

Answer the questions using the Time-Duration expression following the examples below.

Example

去年你學中文學了幾個月？　　　　　我一共學了五個月。

① 你等了多久？　　　　　　　　　　我等了＿＿＿＿＿＿＿＿。

② 你在臺南玩了多久？　　　　　　　我玩了＿＿＿＿＿＿＿＿。

③ 他在臺北住了多久？　　　　　　　他住了＿＿＿＿＿＿＿＿。

④ 你昨天打網球打了幾個鐘頭？　　　我＿＿＿＿＿＿＿＿＿＿。

⑤ 你在紐約住了兩年吧？　　　　　　我＿＿＿＿＿＿＿，只
　　　　　　　　　　　　　　　　　　＿＿＿＿＿＿。（八個月）

⑥ 你昨天看電視看了三個鐘頭，　　　我＿＿＿＿＿＿＿，只
　　對不對？　　　　　　　　　　　　＿＿＿＿＿。（兩個鐘頭）

II. Completion-to-date with Double 了 le 14-06  拼音、英譯 p.90

Function: The Double 了 + Time-Duration pattern indicates the completion of an action up to the time of speaking. The action may or may not continue, depending on the context.

① 她已經在臺灣玩了一年了。

② 陳小姐在美國住了五年了。

③ 我工作了兩個月了。

④ 這間房子，他已經租了半年了。

⑤ 他們學中文學了三個星期了。

練習 Exercise

Answer the questions given using the Double 了 +Time-Duration pattern.

Example

你在語言中心學了多久的中文了？　我學了兩個多月了。

① 你在臺灣工作了多久了？　　　我工作了 ＿＿＿＿＿＿＿。

② 陳老師教了多久的中文了？　　他教了 ＿＿＿＿＿＿＿。

③ 他在那裡住了多久了？　　　　他住了 ＿＿＿＿＿＿＿。

④ 玉山下雪下了多久了？　　　　玉山已經 ＿＿＿＿＿＿＿。

III. 快 kuài⋯了 le *about to* 14-07　　　 拼音、英譯 p.91

Function: The sentential 了 *le* often appears in sentences that contain adverbs indicating "something will soon happen", 快 *kuài*, 要 *yào*, or 快要 *kuài yào*. The 了 *le* suggests an imminent change of state.

① 快下雨了。　　　　　② 電影要結束了。

③ 爸爸快要到家了。

Structures:

 Questions:

① 你媽媽的生日快到了嗎？

② 比賽要開始了嗎？

③ 哥哥的女朋友快要回法國（Fǎguó, France）了嗎？

Usage: This pattern indicates that an action or event will soon happen. In Taiwan, the bi-syllabic 快要 *kuài yào* is preferred. For example, 我的生日快要到了。*Wǒ de shēngrì kuài yào dào le.* "My birthday is coming soon ." If there is a time word, 快要 *kuài yào* can not be used. For example, *他明天快要回來了 Tā míngtiān kuài yào huílái le* "He will be returning tomorrow".

練習 Exercise

Answer the questions referring to the events below that will be happening soon.

① A：你的老師回國了嗎？ B：他_____。大概後天吧！

② A：安同的生日是幾月 B：他的生日_____。
　　幾號？ 下個月一號。

③ A：已經十點了，哥哥怎麼 B：_____。他說五分鐘以
　　還沒來？ 後會到。

④ A：你等一下可以打電話給 B：不行，電影_____開始了。
　　我嗎？

⑤ A：外面風怎麼那麼大？ B：_____下雨了，我們走吧！

IV. Comparison 更 gèng *even more so*   14-08  拼音、英譯 p.91

Function: The adverb 更 presents a fact that is superior to a fact presented in a previous statement. E.g., 星期天我更忙。*Xīngqítiān wǒ gèng máng* means that I am/will be even busier on Sunday than normally. In this lesson, we will introduce sentences in which 更 is used with 比 comparison.

① 他很高，他哥哥比他更高。
② 今年比去年更冷。
③ 我覺得芒果比西瓜更好吃。

Structures: 更 is an adverb that modifies state verbs and is thus placed in front of state verbs.

Questions: The 是不是 pattern is typically used in this structure.

① 這次的颱風是不是比上次的更大？
② 在學校上網是不是比在家裡更快？

練習 Exercise

Describe the following situations using the comparison : even more so with ⋯比⋯更⋯.

❶ 一張火車票賣八百塊錢，
　一張高鐵票要一千五百塊錢。

❷ 安同吃了兩碗牛肉麵，
　明華吃了三碗牛肉麵。

❸ 去年有 35000 人來這裡學中文，
　今年有 52000 人來這裡學中文。

❹ 我學了三年的中文，
　我女朋友學了四年半的中文。

❺ 騎機車去故宮要二十分鐘，
　坐公車去故宮要半個鐘頭。

V. Inferior Comparison 沒有 méi yǒu⋯ 14-09

 拼音、英譯 p.92

Function: The A 沒有 B 那麼／這麼⋯ pattern is used to compare two things A & B and is used to indicate that A is not as (adjective) as B.

❶ 哥哥沒有爸爸那麼高。
❷ 火車沒有高鐵那麼快。
❸ 我的中文沒有老師的那麼好。
❹ 臭豆腐沒有牛肉麵這麼好吃。
❺ 甜點沒有小籠包那麼好做。
❻ 這次的颱風沒有上次的那麼可怕。

Structures: Note that this pattern is usually used in the negative, 沒（有）*méi (yǒu)*. Sometimes, 那麼 *nàme* or 這麼 *zhème* can be omitted. Its positive counterpart, "A 有 *yǒu* B 那麼 *nàme*／ 這麼 *zhème* state verb", is rarely used, except in 嗎 questions.

✏️ **Questions:** The A-not-A pattern is used for questions.

① 妹妹有沒有姐姐那麼漂亮？
② 花蓮的房租有沒有臺北的那麼貴？
③ 日本的工作有沒有美國的那麼難找？
④ 夏天的天氣有沒有春天的舒服？

Usage: This pattern indicates that A is not as (adjective) as B. When A and B are the same, use the "equal degree" pattern introduced in Lesson 13, 'A 跟 *gēn* B 一樣 *yíyàng*...'. The pattern for "superior degree", 'A 比 *bǐ* B…' was introduced in Lesson 8. When you ask a question like 今天有沒有昨天熱？ Is today as hot as yesterday? It is assumed that yesterday was quite hot. Three different responses to the question are possible as shown below:

① 今天跟昨天一樣熱。（equal degree）
② 今天沒有昨天那麼熱。（inferior degree）
③ 今天比昨天熱。（superior degree）

練習 Exercise

Answer the questions given using the A 沒有 B 那麼／這麼… pattern.

Example

哥哥和弟弟，誰比較高？ 　　　　　　哥哥沒有弟弟那麼高。

① 臺北和紐約，哪裡比較冷？ ＿＿＿＿＿＿＿＿＿＿＿。
② 西瓜和芒果，哪種水果比較甜？ ＿＿＿＿＿＿＿＿＿＿＿。
③ 今年的生意好還是去年的好？ ＿＿＿＿＿＿＿＿＿＿＿。
④ 咖啡好喝，還是烏龍茶好喝？ ＿＿＿＿＿＿＿＿＿＿＿。

語法例句拼音與英譯
Grammar Examples in Pinyin and English

I. Time-Duration after verbal 了 le

Function:

① Māma de péngyǒu zài Táiběi wánle sān tiān.
② Lǎoshī zài Měiguó zhùle yì nián.
③ Lǐ Xiǎojiě zài yǔyán zhōngxīn gōngzuòle yí ge yuè.

Structures:

1. (1) Tā zū fángzi zūle bàn nián.
   (2) Tā zhù Táiběi zhùle sān nián.

2. (1) Fángzi tā zhǐ zūle bàn nián.

   (2) Táiběi tā zhǐ zhùle sān nián.

Questions:

① Nà jiān fángzi nǐ zūle yì nián bàn ma?
② Nǐ shìbúshì zài zhèlǐ děngle yí ge zhōngtóu?
③ Chén Lǎobǎn qùnián shìbúshì zài Niǔyuē zhùle bàn nián?

Function:

① My mom's friend visited Taipei for three days (and went back home.)
② Our teacher stayed in the US for a year.
③ Miss. Li worked in the language center for one month (and left).

Structures:

1. (1) He rented the house for half a year.
   (2) He lived in Taipei for three years.

2. (1) He rented the house for only half a year.
   (2) He lived in Taipei for only three years.

Questions:

① Did you rent that house for one and a half years?
② You waited here for an hour, right?
③ The Boss Chen stayed in New York for half a year last year, right?

II. Completion-to-date with Double 了 le

Function:

① Tā yǐjīng zài Táiwān wánle yì nián le.
② Chén Xiǎojiě zài Měiguó zhùle wǔ nián le.
③ Wǒ gōngzuòle liǎng ge yuè le.
④ Zhè jiān fángzi, tā yǐjīng zūle bàn nián le.

⑤ Tāmen xué Zhōngwén xuéle sān ge xīngqí le.

Function:

① She has already been in Taiwan for a year.
② Miss Chen has lived in the US for five years.
③ I've been working for two months.
④ He has been renting this house for half a year.
⑤ They have studied Chinese for three weeks now.

III. 快 kuài···了 le *about to*

Function:

1. Kuài xiàyǔ le.
2. Diànyǐng yào jiéshù le.
3. Bàba kuài yào dào jiā le.

Structures:

🖊 **Questions：**

1. Nǐ māma de shēngrì kuài dàole ma?
2. Bǐsài yào kāishǐle ma?
3. Gēge de nǚ péngyǒu kuài yào huí Fǎguó le ma?

Function:

1. It's going to rain soon.
2. The movie is about to finish.
3. Dad is almost home.

Structures:

🖊 **Questions：**

1. Is your mom's birthday coming soon?
2. Is the game about to start?
3. Is brother's girlfriend going back to France soon?

IV. Comparison 更 gèng *even more so*

Function:

1. Tā hěn gāo, tā gēge bǐ tā gèng gāo.

2. Jīnnián bǐ qùnián gèng lěng.

3. Wǒ juéde mángguǒ bǐ xīguā gèng hǎochī.

Function:

1. He is very tall. His brother is even taller than him.
2. This year is even colder than last year. (Last year was already very cold.)
3. I think mangos are even more delicious than watermelons. (Watermelons are (very) delicious as everyone knows.)

Structures:

🖊 **Questions：**

1. Zhè cì de táifēng shìbúshì bǐ shàng cì de gèng dà?
2. Zài xuéxiào shàngwǎng shìbúshì bǐ zài jiā lǐ gèng kuài?

Structures:

🖊 **Questions：**

1. Is this typhoon bigger than the one last time?
2. Is the internet at school even faster than at home?

V. Inferior Comparison with 沒有 méi yǒu…

Function:

1 Gēge méi yǒu bàba nàme gāo.

2 Huǒchē méi yǒu gāotiě nàme kuài.

3 Wǒ de Zhōngwén méi yǒu lǎoshī de nàme hǎo.

4 Chòu dòufǔ méi yǒu niúròu miàn zhème hǎochī.

5 Tiándiǎn méi yǒu xiǎolóngbāo nàme hǎo zuò.

6 Zhè cì de táifēng méi yǒu shàng cì de nàme kěpà.

Function:

1 My older brother is not as tall as my dad.

2 The train is not as fast as the High Speed Rail.

3 My Chinese is not as good as my teacher's.

4 The stinky tofu is not as good as the beef noodles.

5 Desserts are not as easy to make as xiaolongbao.

6 This typhoon is not as scary as the last one.

Structures:

✏ Questions:

1 Mèimei yǒu méi yǒu jiějie nàme piàoliàng?

2 Huālián de fángzū yǒu méi yǒu Táiběi de nàme guì?

3 Rìběn de gōngzuò yǒu méi yǒu Měiguó de nàme nán zhǎo?

4 Xiàtiān de tiānqì yǒu méi yǒu chūntiān de shūfú?

✏ Questions:

1 Is the younger sister as pretty as the older sister?

2 Is rent in Hualien as expensive as in Taipei?

3 Are jobs in Japan as hard to find as in the US?

4 Is the weather in the summer as pleasant as that in the spring?

Usage:

1 Jīntiān gēn zuótiān yíyàng rè.

2 Jīntiān méi yǒu zuótiān nàme rè.

3 Jīntiān bǐ zuótiān rè.

Usage:

1 Today is as hot as yesterday.

2 Today is not as hot as yesterday.

3 Today is hotter than yesterday.

Classroom Activities

I. The Four Seasons

Goal: Learning to describe the four seasons and explain why one likes or dislikes them.

Task: Tell the class about the climate of your home country. Which season do you like the most and the least. Why?

春天

夏天

秋天

冬天

問 Ask		回答 Answer
春、夏、秋、冬	喜歡嗎？	為什麼？（因為…所以…）
❶ 你喜歡春天嗎？	喜歡 ☐ 不喜歡 ☐	
❷ 你喜歡夏天嗎？	喜歡 ☐ 不喜歡 ☐	
❸ 你喜歡秋天嗎？	喜歡 ☐ 不喜歡 ☐	
❹ 你喜歡冬天嗎？	喜歡 ☐ 不喜歡 ☐	

II. How Long Did You Live There?

Goal: Learning to make simple statemenst about your experiences.

Task: Ask your classmates where they have lived, and how long they lived in each place. Record your findings and report to the class. E.g.,

安同在___西班牙___住了多久？

安同在___西班牙___住了___兩個月（了）___。

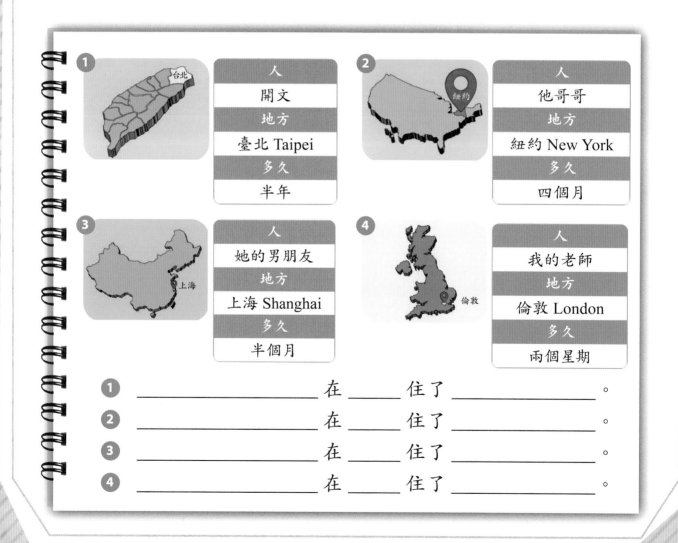

人
開文
地方
臺北 Taipei
多久
半年

人
他哥哥
地方
紐約 New York
多久
四個月

人
她的男朋友
地方
上海 Shanghai
多久
半個月

人
我的老師
地方
倫敦 London
多久
兩個星期

1 ＿＿＿＿＿＿＿ 在 ＿＿＿ 住了 ＿＿＿＿＿＿ 。

2 ＿＿＿＿＿＿＿ 在 ＿＿＿ 住了 ＿＿＿＿＿＿ 。

3 ＿＿＿＿＿＿＿ 在 ＿＿＿ 住了 ＿＿＿＿＿＿ 。

4 ＿＿＿＿＿＿＿ 在 ＿＿＿ 住了 ＿＿＿＿＿＿ 。

III. Temperature Comparison

Goal: Learning to make comparisons between events.

Task: Compare the average temperatures of Taipei in the various seasons of last year and this year. Use the patterns 比、更、比較、比…更、跟…一樣、沒有…那麼 introduced earlier.

臺北

	去年	今年
春	25℃	25℃
夏	36℃	38℃
秋	21℃	20℃
冬	12℃	10℃

註：℃＝度 *dù* （degrees Celsius）

IV. Same Weathers

Goal: Learning to compare weather conditions.

Task: You learned during the first activity what the climate for each of your classmate's country is like. Please compare the climate of one classmate's home country with that of yours. Ask for more information and write the results on the chart below.

你和同學的國家的天氣		
	自己國家的天氣	同學國家的天氣
春天的天氣怎麼樣？		

	自己國家的天氣	同學國家的天氣
夏天的天氣怎麼樣？		
秋天的天氣怎麼樣？		
冬天的天氣怎麼樣？		
有沒有颱風？		
常不常下雨？		
會不會下雪？		

V. Summer in Taiwan

Goal: Learning to discuss events and activities in summer.

Task: Discuss with a classmate and write down your findings in Chinese.

臺灣的夏天 **Summer in Taiwan**	
夏天	有什麼比較特別的…
天氣怎麼樣	
常吃的水果	
常做的事	

文化 *Bits of Chinese Culture*

Typhoon Days-Off

"Typhoon days" are breaks from school and work that are announced when a typhoon with average wind speeds of class 7 or higher or gusts of class 10 or higher is expected to pass through an area sometime within the next four hours. School and work are cancelled until the storm passes.

▲ Typhoon satellite image
資料來源：中央氣象局

Typhoons bring strong winds and heavy rains and the power to decide to cancel work and school was given to the Directorate-General of Personnel Administration in 1993. The DGPA took into consideration weather forecasts from the Central Weather Bureau and suggestions from local governments when deciding whether or not to announce national-wide typhoon days. Today, the DGPA does not decide for the entire nation; instead the decision has been vested to regional governments. To find out whether work and school will be cancelled for a storm, check with the local news or DGPA's official website at http://www.cpa.gov.tw/ or call 020-300-166 for updates.

▲ Damage from a typhoon caused
《聯合報》施鴻基 / 攝影

▲ Typhoon wind and rain
《聯合報》屠惠剛 / 攝影

▲ Taking precautions against a typhoon
《聯合報》劉學聖 / 攝影

Self-Assessment Checklist

I can talk about weather conditions, including typhoons.

20%　　40%　　60%　　80%　　100%

I can describe the four seasons and explain why I like or dislike them.

20%　　40%　　60%　　80%　　100%

I can compare events.

20%　　40%　　60%　　80%　　100%

I can make simple statements about experiences, e.g., trips.

20%　　40%　　60%　　80%　　100%

Note

第十五課

我很不舒服
I Don't Feel Well

學習目標 Learning Objectives

Topic: 生病 Falling Sick

- Learning to ask someone how they are feeling.

- Learning to describe symptoms in simple terms.

- Learning to give suggestions to somebody who is sick.

- Learning to reject or accept suggestions.

我很不舒服

I Don't Feel Well

對話一 Dialogue 1 15-01 AR 15-A

醫　生：白小姐，妳哪裡不舒服？

如　玉：我一直流鼻水，頭很痛，胃口很差。
什麼東西都不想吃。

醫　生：大概多久了？

如　玉：已經四、五天了。

醫　生：我看看妳的喉嚨。喉嚨有一點發炎。

如　玉：請問我生的是什麼病？

醫　生：妳有一點發燒，是感冒，不過沒有什麼關係。

如　玉：請問我得吃藥嗎？

醫　生：要，妳到藥局去拿藥。

如　　玉：好的。請問我的病什麼時候會好？

醫　　生：回去把藥吃了，多喝水，多休息，早一點
　　　　　睡覺，很快就會好。

如　　玉：好的，謝謝您。

課文拼音 Text in Pinyin

Yīshēng : Bái Xiǎojiě, nǐ nǎlǐ bù shūfú?

Rúyù : Wǒ yìzhí liú bíshuǐ, tóu hěn tòng, wèikǒu hěn chā. Shénme dōngxi dōu bù
xiǎng chī.

Yīshēng : Dàgài duō jiǔ le?

Rúyù : Yǐjīng sì, wǔtiān le.

Yīshēng : Wǒ kànkàn nǐ de hóulóng. Hóulóng yǒu yìdiǎn fāyán.

Rúyù : Qǐngwèn wǒ shēng de shì shénme bìng?

Yīshēng : Nǐ yǒu yìdiǎn fāshāo, shì gǎnmào, búguò méi yǒu shénme guānxi.

Rúyù : Qǐngwèn wǒ děi chī yào ma?

Yīshēng : Yào, nǐ dào yàojú qù ná yào.

Rúyù : Hǎode. Qǐngwèn wǒ de bìng shénme shíhòu huì hǎo?

Yīshēng : Huíqù bǎ yào chīle, duō hē shuǐ, duō xiūxí, zǎo yìdiǎn shuìjiào, hěn kuài jiù huì hǎo.

Rúyù : Hǎode, xièxie nín.

課文英譯 Text in English

Doctor : Miss Bai, how are you doing? (Where are you feeling poorly?)

Ruyu : My nose continues to run, my head aches, and my appetite is poor. I don't feel
like eating anything.

Doctor : About how long?

Ruyu : About four or five days now.

Doctor	: Let me take a look at your throat. Your throat is a bit inflamed.
Ruyu	: Excuse me, what sickness do I have?
Doctor	: You have a slight fever. It is a cold, but it's nothing serious.
Ruyu	: Excuse me, do I have to take any medicine?
Doctor	: Yes. Go to the pharmacy to pick up your medicine.
Ruyu	: Thank you. Excuse me, when will I be well again?
Doctor	: Go home, take your medicine, drink plenty of water, get plenty of rest, and go to bed early and you'll be better very soon.
Ruyu	: Fine, thank you.

生詞一 Vocabulary 1 15-02

Vocabulary

1	醫生	yīshēng	ㄧ ㄕㄥ	(N)	doctor
2	一直	yìzhí	ㄧˊ ㄓˊ	(Adv)	continuously, all the way
3	流	liú	ㄌㄧㄡˊ	(V)	to flow
4	鼻水	bíshuǐ	ㄅㄧˊ ㄕㄨㄟˇ	(N)	snot, nasal mucus, a running nose
5	頭	tóu	ㄊㄡˊ	(N)	head
6	痛	tòng	ㄊㄨㄥˋ	(Vs)	painful
7	胃口	wèikǒu	ㄨㄟˋ ㄎㄡˇ	(N)	appetite
8	差	chā	ㄔㄚ	(Vs)	poor, bad
9	喉嚨	hóulóng	ㄏㄡˊ ㄌㄨㄥˊ	(N)	throat
10	發炎	fāyán	ㄈㄚ ㄧㄢˊ	(Vp-sep)	to be inflamed
11	生病	shēngbìng	ㄕㄥ ㄅㄧㄥˋ	(Vp-sep)	to fall ill
12	發燒	fāshāo	ㄈㄚ ㄕㄠ	(Vp-sep)	to have a fever
13	感冒	gǎnmào	ㄍㄢˇ ㄇㄠˋ	(Vp)	to catch/have a cold
14	藥	yào	ㄧㄠˋ	(N)	medicine
15	藥局	yàojú	ㄧㄠˋ ㄐㄩˊ	(N)	pharmacy, drug store
16	拿	ná	ㄋㄚˊ	(V)	to get

17	把	bǎ	ㄅㄚˇ	(Ptc)	disposal marker
18	水	shuǐ	ㄕㄨㄟˇ	(N)	water
19	休息	xiūxí	ㄒㄧㄡ ㄒㄧˊ	(Vi)	to take a rest
20	睡覺	shuìjiào	ㄕㄨㄟˋ ㄐㄧㄠˋ	(V-sep)	to sleep

Phrases

| 21 | 早一點 | zǎo yìdiǎn | ㄗㄠˇ ㄧˋ ㄉㄧㄢˇ | | a bit earlier |

對話二 Dialogue 2 　🎧 15-03　AR 15-B

如　玉：你怎麼了？臉色這麼難看。

安　同：昨天晚上肚子很不舒服，吃了東西就吐，
　　　　還吐了好幾次。

如　玉：你這麼不舒服，我陪你去看病，好不好？

安　同：不用了。我在臺灣沒有健康保險。

如　玉：那麼，我陪你去學校的健康中心。那裡的醫生很好，對學生也很客氣。

安　同：謝謝妳。我想去藥局買藥就好了。

如　玉：你真的不去看病嗎？

安　同：我想回家休息。請妳跟老師說，我生病了，不能上課。

如　玉：好。你自己要多小心。油的、冰的東西最好都別吃。

安　同：謝謝妳的關心。

（如玉下課以後）

如　玉：我來看你了。現在覺得怎麼樣？好一點了嗎？

安　同：謝謝妳，好多了。我吃了一包藥以後，睡得比昨天好。

如　玉：不錯。你睡了幾個小時的覺以後，現在臉色比早上好得多了。

課文拼音 Text in Pinyin

Rúyù ：Nǐ zěnme le? Liǎnsè zhème nánkàn.

Āntóng ：Zuótiān wǎnshàng dùzi hěn bù shūfú, chīle dōngxi jiù tù, hái tùle hǎo jǐ cì.

Rúyù ：Nǐ zhème bù shūfú, wǒ péi nǐ qù kànbìng, hǎo bù hǎo?

Āntóng ：Búyòng le. Wǒ zài Táiwān méi yǒu jiànkāng bǎoxiǎn.

Rúyù ：Nàme, wǒ péi nǐ qù xuéxiào de jiànkāng zhōngxīn. Nàlǐ de yīshēng hěn hǎo, duì xuéshēng yě hěn kèqì.

Āntóng ：Xièxie nǐ. Wǒ xiǎng qù yàojú mǎi yào jiù hǎo le.

Rúyù ：Nǐ zhēnde bú qù kànbìng ma?

Āntóng ：Wǒ xiǎng huí jiā xiūxí. Qǐng nǐ gēn lǎoshī shuō, wǒ shēngbìng le, bù néng shàngkè.

| Rúyù | : Hǎo. Nǐ zìjǐ yào duō xiǎoxīn. Yóu de, bīng de dōngxi zuìhǎo dōu bié chī. |
| Āntóng | : Xièxie nǐ de guānxīn. |

[Rúyù xiàkè yǐhòu]

Rúyù	: Wǒ lái kàn nǐ le. Xiànzài juéde zěnmeyàng? Hǎo yìdiǎn le ma?
Āntóng	: Xièxie nǐ, hǎo duō le. Wǒ chīle yì bāo yào yǐhòu, shuì de bǐ zuótiān hǎo.
Rúyù	: Búcuò. Nǐ shuìle jǐ ge xiǎoshí de jiào yǐhòu, xiànzài liǎnsè bǐ zǎoshàng hǎo de duō le.

课文英譯 Text in English

Ruyu	: What's the matter? You don't look too good.
Antong	: My stomach didn't feel good last night. I ate something and then threw up. I vomited several times.
Ruyu	: You're feeling that badly. I'll go with you to see a doctor. Okay?
Antong	: No need. I don't have health insurance in Taiwan.
Ruyu	: Then I'll go with you to the school's health center. The doctors there are good, and they are polite to students.
Antong	: Thank you. I think I'll just buy some medicine at a drug store. That should do it.
Ruyu	: You're really not going to see a doctor?
Antong	: I just want to go home and rest. Please tell the teacher I am sick and I can't go to class.
Ruyu	: Take care of yourself. You'd best not eat anything oily or cold.
Antong	: Thank you for your concern.

[after Ruyu gets out of class]

Ruyu	: I came to see you. How are you feeling now? Any better?
Antong	: Thanks. Much better now. I took a packet of medicine and slept a lot better than yesterday.
Ruyu	: Good. After having slept for a few hours, you now look much better than this morning.

生詞二 Vocabulary 🎧 15-04

Vocabulary

1	臉色	liǎnsè	ㄌㄧㄢˇ ㄙㄜˋ	(N)	a person's "color" (said of the face when healthy or sick, pleased or angry etc.)
2	難看	nánkàn	ㄋㄢˊ ㄎㄢˋ	(Vs)	not to look good
3	肚子	dùzi	ㄉㄨˋ ㄗ˙	(N)	stomach, abdomen
4	吐	tù	ㄊㄨˋ	(V)	to throw up, to vomit
5	幾	jǐ	ㄐㄧˇ	(N)	(a) few
6	次	cì	ㄘˋ	(M)	measure word for times, occurrences
7	陪	péi	ㄆㄟˊ	(V)	to go/stay with somebody, to accompany
8	看病	kànbìng	ㄎㄢˋ ㄅㄧㄥˋ	(V-sep)	to see a doctor
9	健康	jiànkāng	ㄐㄧㄢˋ ㄎㄤ	(N)	health
10	保險	bǎoxiǎn	ㄅㄠˇ ㄒㄧㄢˇ	(N)	insurance
11	跟	gēn	ㄍㄣ	(Prep)	to
12	油	yóu	ㄧㄡˊ	(Vs)	oily, greasy
13	冰	bīng	ㄅㄧㄥ	(Vs)	icy
14	別	bié	ㄅㄧㄝˊ	(Adv)	don't (used in imperatives)
15	關心	guānxīn	ㄍㄨㄢ ㄒㄧㄣ	(Vst)	to be concerned about
16	包	bāo	ㄅㄠ	(M)	measure word for bags, packages etc.
17	睡	shuì	ㄕㄨㄟˋ	(Vi)	to sleep
18	小時	xiǎoshí	ㄒㄧㄠˇ ㄕˊ	(N)	hour

Phrases

19	怎麼了	zěnme le	ㄗㄣˇ ㄇㄜ˙ ㄌㄜ˙		What's wrong?
20	不用了	búyòng le	ㄅㄨˊ ㄩㄥˋ ㄌㄜ˙		It's not necessary.
21	健康中心	jiànkāng zhōngxīn	ㄐㄧㄢˋ ㄎㄤ ㄓㄨㄥ ㄒㄧㄣ		health center

| 22 | 回家 | huí jiā | ㄏㄨㄟˊ ㄐㄧㄚ | go home |
| 23 | 最好 | zuìhǎo | ㄗㄨㄟˋ ㄏㄠˇ | It would be best.../ (You) should... |

文法 Grammar

I. Non-committal Stance with Question Words 15-05  拼音、英譯 p.118

Function: When question words（e.g., 什麼 *shénme*, 多少 *duōshǎo*, 幾 *jǐ*, 哪裡 *nǎlǐ*, 什麼地方 *shénme dìfāng*, 誰 *shéi*, 什麼時候 *shénme shíhòu*）occur in a declarative sentence, the sentence indicates a non-committal attitude on the part of the speaker who is avoiding giving a clear answer. Non-committal statements are always in the negative.

❶ 我沒有多少錢。　　　❷ 她沒有幾個朋友。

❸ 你的感冒沒有什麼關係。　❹ 我沒去哪裡。

❺ 他不打算買什麼。　　　❻ 我昨天沒跟誰去看電影。

練習 Exercise

Answer the question using with question words indicating a non-committal attitude.

問 Ask	答 Answer
❶ 你的房租一個月多少錢？	沒有多少錢。
❷ 週末快到了，你打算去哪裡玩？	我 ＿＿＿＿＿＿＿＿＿＿。
❸ 你在看什麼？	我 ＿＿＿＿＿＿＿＿＿＿。
❹ 你在臺灣有很多朋友嗎？	我 ＿＿＿＿＿＿＿＿＿＿。
❺ 你昨天去便利商店買了什麼東西？	我昨天 ＿＿＿＿＿＿＿＿。

II. To Dispose of Something with 把 bǎ 15-06

Function: This pattern is generally referred to as 把 *bǎ* or disposal construction . It consists of a variety of internal elements and is quite similar to the phrase "take this (noun) and..." in English, but much more widely used. We begin with the most basic structure, which refers to how a noun, object of the action verb, is disposed of by the subject.

❶ 我把牛肉麵吃了。   ❷ 他把我的湯喝了。

❸ 房東把房子賣了。

Structures: 把 *bǎ* + object + verb + 了 *le*, in which the object is in most cases definite in reference (bare nouns, or nouns with modifiers such as 這個, 那個, 他的, etc.), the verb (bare, i.e., just one character) must be an outward transitive action verb (action away from the actor, not inward towards the actor), and sentence must end with the particle 了 .

✏ **Negation:** The negation uses 沒 or 別 occurs in front of the particle 把 *bǎ*.

❶ 我沒把豬腳麵線吃了。   ❷ 別把我的藥吃了。

❸ 他沒把書賣了。

✏ **Questions:**

❶ 你把功課寫了沒有？   ❷ 你是不是把機車賣了？

❸ 你是不是把他的早飯吃了？

Usage:

1. As mentioned above, the object of 把 *bǎ* must be definite.

   (1) 我想把手機賣了。

   (2) 我想把那支手機賣了。

        *我想把一支手機賣了。

2. As also mentioned earlier, the bare verb in 把 *bǎ* sentences must be outward and transitive. They include 賣 *mài*, 吃 *chī*, 喝 *hē*, 寫 *xiě*, but not such inward verbs as 買 *mǎi*, 學 *xué*. You cannot say *我把中文學了 .

3. The notion "dispose of" is often indicated using "do-with", "do-to", and "take (noun) and (verb)" in English, e.g., "What he did with his car was to sell it" or "He took his car and sold it."

練習 Exercise

According to the pictures below, what did the individuals do with the coffee, book, xiaolongbao, beef noodles, and motorcycle?

她 ＿＿＿＿＿＿＿＿＿。

王先生 ＿＿＿＿＿＿＿＿。

她 ＿＿＿＿＿＿＿＿＿。

她 ＿＿＿＿＿＿＿＿＿。

老闆 ＿＿＿＿＿＿＿＿＿。

III. V 了 le… 就 jiù… *do…right after doing…* 🎧 15-07   🔍拼音、英譯 p.119

Function: The pattern "V 了…就…" indicates that event 2 occurs right after the completion of event 1.

❶ 我放了假就去旅行。 **❷** 他吃了藥就睡覺。

❸ 爸爸回了家就喝了兩杯烏龍茶。

Structures: The two events can be in the affirmative or negative.

❶ 他到了臺北，就去臺北 101 看看。

❷ 妹妹喝了一碗熱湯，就不覺得冷了。

❸ 姐姐吃了臭豆腐，肚子就不舒服。

✏ Questions:

The A-not-A form is not possible. Either 嗎 *ma* or 是不是 *shìbúshì* can be used to form questions.

① 他們見了面，就去喝咖啡嗎？

② 你弟弟是不是下了課，就去 KTV 唱歌？

③ 他是不是去紐約玩了兩個星期，就不想回來了？

Usage: The "V 了…就…" pattern taught in this lesson is similar to the "一…就" in Lesson 13, but differs as explained below:

1. The "一" is followed by a relatively short verbal phrase, e.g., 一出來就… and 一看就…, to emphasize the immediate succession of the two actions. In contrast, the "V 了" pattern is not as restricted in terms of what can follow it.

2. "以後" can be used with "V 了…就…", but it cannot with the "一…就" pattern.

他吃了藥以後，就去睡覺。

*他一吃了藥以後，就去睡覺。

練習 Exercise

Complete the following dialogues using the V 了…就… pattern.

① A：你什麼時候買禮物？　　B：_____。
（訂蛋糕）

② A：你什麼時候可以看足球　B：_____。
比賽？　　　　　　　（裝有線電視）

③ A：你什麼時候去日本旅行？B：_____。
（放假）

④ A：你什麼時候開始上課？　B：_____。，
（付學費）

⑤ A：他什麼時候回來？　　　B：_____。
（看紅葉）

IV. 一點 yìdiǎn *a bit* 🎧 15-08

拼音、英譯 p.120

Function: The combination 一點 *yìdiǎn* indicates a minimal quantity or degree.

❶ 他喝了一點咖啡。

❷ 這一點錢太少了。

❸ 她要吃一點麵線。

Structures: 一點 *yìdiǎn* can appear in a variety of structures as illustrated below.

1. 一點＋NP: Before a noun as its modifier.

    (1) 她在超市買了一點東西。　　**(2)** 我只喝了一點烏龍茶。

    (3) 昨天下了一點雨。

2. Vs＋一點: After a state verb as its modifier, it indicates comparison, as in "a little more/less...".

    (1) 他比我年輕一點。　　**(2)** 請你早一點來！

    (3) 明天我會晚一點回家。

3. 有(一)點＋Vs: Before a state verb but preceded by 有 as a modifier of the adjective, it doesn't indicate comparison.

    (1) 牛肉麵有一點辣。　　**(2)** 這裡，冬天有一點冷。

    (3) 這支手機有一點貴。　　**(4)** 他有(一)點想睡。

Usage: 一點 can be reduplicated to form 一點點, indicating that something is "just a tiny bit", e.g., 我只要一點點。 Wǒ zhǐ yào yìdiǎndiǎn. "I just want a little bit."

練習 Exercise

Complete the sentences below using the minimal quantity expression 一點.

Example 他給我的太少了，我希望他多給我一點。

❶ A：你不舒服，吃飯了沒有？

    B：我只 ＿＿＿＿＿＿＿＿＿（喝湯）。

❷ 你感冒了，最好 ＿＿＿＿＿＿＿＿＿（睡覺）。

③ 今天下午有籃球比賽，我們都很想看，請問老師能不能
　　＿＿＿＿＿＿＿（早）下課？

④ 我明天要看網球比賽，會 ＿＿＿＿＿＿＿（晚）回家。

練習 Exercise

Complete the sentences below using 一點 *yìdiǎn,* 有一點 *yǒu yìdiǎn,* or 多 *duō* /
少 *shǎo* V 一點 *yìdiǎn.*

① 他昨天工作了十個鐘頭，覺得 ＿＿＿＿＿＿＿ 累。

② 我感冒了，喉嚨 ＿＿＿＿＿＿＿ 發炎。

③ 今天不上班，早上我想 ＿＿＿＿＿＿＿ 覺。

④ 媽媽想去超市買 ＿＿＿＿＿＿＿ 東西。

⑤ 我租的房子很好，可是房租 ＿＿＿＿＿＿＿ 貴。

⑥ 今年的學費比去年貴，我要 ＿＿＿＿＿＿＿ 衣服。

⑦ 這碗臭豆腐 ＿＿＿＿＿＿＿（辣），我不想吃。

V. Comparing Actions with a 得 de Complement　🎧 15-09　🔍 拼音、英譯 p.120

Function: This pattern compares actions.

① 哥哥吃牛肉麵吃得比弟弟多。　　② 這種手機賣得比那種好。

Structures: The pattern is called "comparative adverbial". The pattern comes in a
variety of sub-patterns as illustrated below.

1. Comparative + Action + 得 + State
   (1) 他比我做得快。　　　　　　(2) 我比他走得快。
   (3) 弟弟比哥哥念得好。

2. Action + 得 + Comparative + State (verb repeated)
   (1) 他做飯做得比我快。　　　　(2) 我走路走得比他快。
   (3) 弟弟念書念得比哥哥好。

Pattern 2 above is used most frequently.

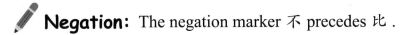 **Negation:** The negation marker 不 precedes 比 .

1 他做飯不比我做得快。

2 走路，我不比他走得快。

3 弟弟念書念得不比哥哥好。

Questions:

1 你做飯做得比媽媽好嗎？

2 他是不是走路走得比你快？

3 弟弟打網球打得比哥哥好嗎？

練習 Exercise

Compare the actions using 得 *de* and complete the following sentences.

Example

我做豬腳麵線要花一個半鐘頭。　　　我做豬腳麵線
我做牛肉麵要花一個鐘頭。　　　　　<u>做得比牛肉麵慢</u>　　。

1 咖啡，今天賣了一百二十杯。　　　今天咖啡
　　烏龍茶，今天賣了八十四杯。　　　＿＿＿＿＿＿＿＿。

2 今年下雪下了三個半月。　　　　　今年下雪
　　去年下雪下了半個月。　　　　　　＿＿＿＿＿＿＿＿。

3 上個週末在 KTV 唱歌唱了五個鐘頭。　這個週末在 KTV 唱歌
　　這個週末在 KTV 唱歌唱了四個鐘頭。　＿＿＿＿＿＿＿＿。

4 媽媽走路走得很快。從家裡到捷運站　媽媽走路＿＿＿＿＿＿
　　要二十分鐘。　　　　　　　　　　不比＿＿＿＿＿＿＿＿。
　　姐姐只要十分鐘。

VI. Complements of Degree in Comparison Structures

拼音、英譯 p.121

🎧 15-10

Function: Degrees can be presented either as a pre-verbal adverbial, or as post-verbal complement. In this lesson, we focus on the latter type, …一點 *yìdiǎn*，…得多 *de duō*，…多了 *duō le*.

❶ 他的房間比我的大一點。

❷ 捷運站比公車站遠得多。

❸ 我覺得晚上比早上舒服多了。

Structures:

🖊 **Questions：**

❶ 哥哥是不是比弟弟高一點？

❷ 房租可以便宜一點嗎？

❸ 春天去旅行是不是比夏天舒服得多？

❹ 高鐵票比火車票貴多了嗎？

練習 Exercise

Answer the questions below using 一點 *yìdiǎn*, 得多 *de duō* and 多了 *duō le* in the complements.

問 Ask	答 Answer
Example 高鐵比公車快嗎？	高鐵比公車快得多／快多了。
❶ 西瓜比芒果大嗎？	＿＿＿＿＿＿＿＿＿＿。
❷ 安同和田中誰打網球打得好？（安同）	＿＿＿＿＿＿＿＿＿＿。
❸ 便利商店的東西貴還是超市的東西貴？	＿＿＿＿＿＿＿＿＿＿。
❹ 姐姐和妹妹誰玩得開心？（妹妹）	＿＿＿＿＿＿＿＿＿＿。

VII. Separable Verbs 15-11

拼音、英譯 p.122

Function: This is a special category of verbs. The inherent structure of most separable verbs is [V+N]. The V and N can be separated and an element inserted in between them. The separated V and N behave like a verb and object. Examples of separable verbs are: 唱歌, 上班, 上網, 上課, 生病, 睡覺, 看書, 念書, 滑雪, 游泳, 照相, 吃飯, 做飯, 見面.

Structures: Basically, there are three types of separable forms. Let's take the words introduced in this volume as examples.

1. 了 inserted. The 了 is the Verbal 了 here.
    (1) 他回了家以後，就開始工作。
    (2) 我昨天下了課就跟朋友去看電影。

2. Object inserted. Object refers to the recipient of an action.
    (1) 我想見你一面。
    (2) 他照了你一張相。

3. Time-Duration inserted.
    (1) 我們每天上八個鐘頭的班。
    (2) 你們新年的時候，放幾天的假？
    (3) 他唱了三小時的歌，有一點累。

練習 Exercise

Separate the elements V and N below, and then insert something in between them to form good sentences.

① 看書 → 看了三小時的書、看了很久的書
② 唱歌 →
③ 上班 →
④ 上網 →
⑤ 上課 →
⑥ 生病 →

⑦	睡覺	→
⑧	念書	→
⑨	滑雪	→
⑩	游泳	→
⑪	照相	→
⑫	吃飯	→
⑬	做飯	→
⑭	見面	→

語法例句拼音與英譯
Grammar Examples in Pinyin and English

I. Non-committal Stance with Question Words

Function:

❶ Wǒ méi yǒu duōshǎo qián.
❷ Tā méi yǒu jǐ ge péngyǒu.

❸ Nǐ de gǎnmào méi yǒu shénme guānxi.
❹ Wǒ méi qù nǎlǐ.
❺ Tā bù dǎsuàn mǎi shénme.
❻ Wǒ zuótiān méi gēn shéi qù kàn diànyǐng.

Function:

❶ I don't really have all that much money.
❷ She doesn't really have all that many friends.
❸ Your cold really isn't all that serious.
❹ I didn't really go anywhere.
❺ He is not going to buy anything.
❻ I really didn't go with anyone to see a movie yesterday.

II. To Dispose of Something with 把 bǎ

Function:

❶ Wǒ bǎ niúròu miàn chī le.

❷ Tā bǎ wǒ de tāng hē le.
❸ Fángdōng bǎ fángzi mài le.

Function:

❶ I ate the beef noodles. (I took the beef noodles and ate them.)
❷ He drank my soup.
❸ The landlord sold the house.

Structures:

Negation:

1. Wǒ méi bǎ zhūjiǎo miànxiàn chī le.
2. Bié bǎ wǒ de yào chī le.
3. Tā méi bǎ shū mài le.

Questions:

1. Nǐ bǎ gōngkè xiěle méi yǒu?
2. Nǐ shìbúshì bǎ jīchē mài le?
3. Nǐ shìbúshì bǎ tā de zǎofàn chī le?

Usage:

1. (1) Wǒ xiǎng bǎ shǒujī mài le.
   (2) Wǒ xiǎng bǎ nà zhī shǒujī mài le.

Structures:

Negation:

1. I didn't eat the pork knuckles with fine noodles.
2. Don't take my medicine.
3. He didn't sell the book.

Questions:

1. Have you finished your homework?
2. You sold the motorcycle, right?
3. You ate his breakfast, right?

Usage:

1. (1) I want to sell my mobile phone.
   (2) I want to sell that mobile phon

III. V 了 le… 就 jiù… *do…right after doing…*

Function:

1. Wǒ fàngle jià jiù qù lǚxíng.
2. Tā chīle yào jiù shuìjiào.
3. Bàba huíle jiā jiù hēle liǎng bēi Wūlóng chá.

Structures:

1. Tā dàole Táiběi, jiù qù Táiběi 101 kànkàn.
2. Mèimei hēle yì wǎn rè tāng, jiù bù juéde lěng le.
3. Jiějie chīle chòu dòufǔ, dùzi jiù bù shūfú.

Questions:

1. Tāmen jiànle miàn, jiù qù hē kāfēi ma?
2. Nǐ dìdi shìbúshì xiàle kè, jiù qù KTV chànggē?
3. Tā shìbúshì qù Niǔyuē wánle liǎng ge xīngqí, jiù bù xiǎng huílái le?

Function:

1. I went on break (my break started) and I went traveling.
2. He took medicine and went to sleep.
3. Dad got home and drank two cups of Oolong tea.

Structures:

1. He arrived in Taipei and checked out Taipei 101.
2. My little sister stopped feeling cold right after she had a bowl of hot soup.
3. Sister ate stinky tofu then her stomach started acting up.

Questions:

1. Did they go to drink coffee after they met?
2. Your brother went to KTV to sing after class, right?
3. He visited New York for two weeks and didn't want to come back, right?

Usage:

2. Tā chīle yào yǐhòu, jiù qù shuìjiào.

Usage:

2. After he took his medicine, he went to bed.

IV. 一點 yìdiǎn *a bit*

Function:

❶ Tā hēle yìdiǎn kāfēi.
❷ Zhè yìdiǎn qián tài shǎo le.
❸ Tā yào chī yìdiǎn miànxiàn.

Function:

❶ He drank a little coffee.
❷ This tiny amount of money is too little.
❸ She wants to eat a little bit of fine noodles.

Structures:

1. (1) Tā zài chāoshì mǎile yìdiǎn dōngxi.
   (2) Wǒ zhǐ hēle yìdiǎn Wūlóng chá.
   (3) Zuótiān xiàle yìdiǎn yǔ.

2. (1) Tā bǐ wǒ niánqīng yìdiǎn.
   (2) Qǐng nǐ zǎo yìdiǎn lái!
   (3) Míngtiān wǒ huì wǎn yìdiǎn huí jiā.

3. (1) Niúròu miàn yǒu yìdiǎn là.
   (2) Zhèlǐ, dōngtiān yǒu yìdiǎn lěng.
   (3) Zhè zhī shǒujī yǒu yìdiǎn guì.
   (4) Tā yǒu (yì) diǎn xiǎng shuì.

Structures:

1. (1) She bought some things at the supermarket.
   (2) I only drank a little Oolong tea.
   (3) It rained a little yesterday.

2. (1) He is a little bit younger than I am.
   (2) Please arrive a little early.
   (3) I'll be home a little later tomorrow.

3. (1) The beef noodles is a little spicy.
   (2) Here, the winters are a bit cold.
   (3) This cell phone is a little expensive.
   (4) He is a little sleepy.

V. Comparing Actions with a 得 de Complement

Function:

❶ Gēge chī niúròu miàn chī de bǐ dìdi duō.

❷ Zhè zhǒng shǒujī mài de bǐ nà zhǒng hǎo.

Function:

❶ The older brother eats more beef noodles than the younger brother.

❷ This type of cell phone sells better than that type.

Structures:

1. (1) Tā bǐ wǒ zuò de kuài.
   (2) Wǒ bǐ tā zǒu de kuài.
   (3) Dìdi bǐ gēge niàn de hǎo.

2. (1) Tā zuòfàn zuò de bǐ wǒ kuài.
   (2) Wǒ zǒulù zǒu de bǐ tā kuài.
   (3) Dìdi niànshū niàn de bǐ gēge hǎo.

Structures:

1. (1) He does it faster than I do.
   (2) I walk faster than he does.
   (3) The younger brother studies better than (is a better student than) his older brother.

2. (1) He cooks faster than I do.
   (2) I walk faster than he does.
   (3) The younger brother studies better than his older brother.

Negation:

1. Tā zuòfàn bù bǐ wǒ zuò de kuài.
2. Zǒulù, wǒ bù bǐ tā zǒu de kuài.
3. Dìdi niànshū niàn de bù bǐ gēge hǎo.

Questions:

1. Nǐ zuòfàn zuò de bǐ māma hǎo ma?
2. Tā shìbúshì zǒulù zǒu de bǐ nǐ kuài?
3. Dìdi dǎ wǎngqiú dǎ de bǐ gēge hǎo ma?

Negation:

1. He doesn't cook faster than I do.
2. I don't walk faster than he does.
3. The younger brother doesn't study better than his older brother.

Questions:

1. Do you cook better than Mom?
2. Does he walk faster than you do?
3. Does the younger brother play tennis better than the older brother?

VI. Complements of Degree in Comparison Structures

Function:

1. Tā de fángjiān bǐ wǒ de dà yìdiǎn.
2. Jiéyùnzhàn bǐ gōngchēzhàn yuǎn de duō.
3. Wǒ juéde wǎnshàng bǐ zǎoshàng shūfú duō le.

Structures:

Questions:

1. Gēge shìbúshì bǐ dìdi gāo yìdiǎn?
2. Fángzū kěyǐ piányí yìdiǎn ma?
3. Chūntiān qù lǚxíng shìbúshì bǐ xiàtiān shūfú de duō?
4. Gāotiě piào bǐ huǒchē piào guì duō le ma?

Function:

1. His room is just a little bigger than mine.
2. The MRT station is much farther away than the bus stop.
3. I think evenings are a lot more comfortable than mornings.

Structures:

Questions:

1. Is the older brother a bit taller than his younger brother?
2. Can the rent be a little cheaper?
3. It is much more enjoyable (lit. comfortable) to travel in the spring than in the summer, isn't it?
4. Are HSR tickets much more expensive than train tickets?

VII. Separable Verbs

Structures:

1. (1) Tā huíle jiā yǐhòu, jiù kāishǐ gōngzuò.
   (2) Wǒ zuótiān xiàle kè jiù gēn péngyǒu qù kàn diànyǐng.

2. (1) Wǒ xiǎng jiàn nǐ yí miàn.
   (2) Tā zhàole nǐ yì zhāng xiàng.

3. (1) Wǒmen měi tiān shàng bā ge zhōngtóu de bān.
   (2) Nǐmen xīnnián de shíhòu, fàng jǐ tiān de jià?
   (3) Tā chàngle sān xiǎoshí de gē, yǒu yìdiǎn lèi.

Structures:

1. (1) He started working after he got home.
   (2) I went to see a movie with friends after class yesterday.

2. (1) I want to meet with you once.
   (2) He took a picture of you.

3. (1) We work eight hours a day.

   (2) How many days do you get off for New Year's?
   (3) He sang for three hours and is a little tired.

課室活動 Classroom Activities

I. Let's Compare

Goal: Learning to make comparisons of varying degrees.

Task: The following four students are learning Chinese in Taipei. They always eat together and go out together, but they don't live together. Please compare the four individuals using the questions in the column on the far left.

	田中	如玉	安同	月美
晚飯吃幾碗	兩碗	一碗半	兩碗半	半碗
房租	NT $ 18,000	NT $ 6,500	NT $ 15,000	NT $ 6,200
怎麼去臺南玩	計程車（三個半小時）	火車（四個半小時）	機車（八個小時）	高鐵（一個小時四十分鐘）

1. 吃晚飯
   (1) 田中吃飯吃得比 ＿＿＿＿＿＿ 吃得 ＿＿＿＿＿＿ 。
   (2) 月美吃得比 ＿＿＿＿＿＿＿＿＿＿＿＿＿＿＿＿ 。
   (3) 如玉吃得 ＿＿＿＿＿＿ 比田中多。

2. 房租
   (1) 月美的房租 ＿＿＿＿＿＿ 如玉的房租 ＿＿＿＿＿＿ 貴。
   (2) 安同的房租很貴，可是田中的比他的 ＿＿＿＿＿＿ 貴，田中的房租比月美的 ＿＿＿＿ ＿＿＿＿ ＿＿＿＿ 。
   (3) 如玉的房租 ＿＿＿＿＿＿ 比月美的便宜。

3. 怎麼去臺南玩

    (1) 如玉坐火車／田中坐計程車 _____。

    (2) 安同騎機車／月美坐高鐵 _____。

    (3) 如玉坐火車／安同騎機車 _____。

II. Who Is Taking Care of Me?

Goal: Learning to ask how someone is feeling and giving suggestions to somebody who is sick.

Task 1: Play the roles A and B below with a classmate and write down your conversation.

Example

    A：你怎麼了？

    B：我喉嚨發炎。

    A：你應該／最好 _____。
      （看病、多休息、早一點睡覺、多喝水）

    B：好的，謝謝你的關心。

李開明

陳文同

王先生

❶ （同意建議 Agreeing to a suggestion）

    A：老李，你怎麼了？

    B：我 _____。

A：你應該／最好 _____ 。

B：好的。

② （同意建議 Agreeing to a suggestion）

A：小陳，你怎麼了？

B：我 _____ 。

A：你應該／最好 _____ 。

B：謝謝你。

③ （拒絕建議 Refusing a suggestion）

A：王先生，你怎麼了？

B：我 _____ 。

A：你應該／最好 _____ 。

B：謝謝你的關心。_____ 。

Task 2: Role-play as a patient. You vomited after dinner last night, and your stomach is upset. You go see a doctor. Your partner is to role-play as the doctor. Describe your symptoms to the doctor. The doctor is to then give some advice.

III. Taking Medication

Goal: Learning to read the instructions on prescriptions.

Task: Look at the prescription below and ask the following three questions.

① 這種藥一天吃幾次？

② 什麼時候吃？

③ 裡面有幾包藥？

IV. Use 把 Construction

Goal: Learning to use the disposal construction 把 .

Task: Form groups of two and ask each group to complete the following dialogues based on the pictures provided.

1 A：加油！我們今天一定要 _____ 這 50 個小籠包 _____ 了。

B：好的，沒有問題。

2 A：要是你 _____ 今天的功課 _____ 了，就可以去打籃球。

B：太好了。

3 A：誰 _____ 我的西瓜 _____ 了？

B：對不起，我不知道是你的。

V. How Are You Feeling?

Goal: Learning to talk about having a cold.

Task: Your friend 如玉 is sick at home. Call her and find out how she is feeling. Ask also four questions about her condition.

1 _____ ?

2 _____ ?

3 _____ ?

4 _____ ?

文化 *Bits of Chinese Culture*

Wearing Surgical Masks

You see people wearing surgical masks. Are they ill? Probably not. People in Taiwan wear surgical masks as a preventative measure among other reasons.

When the seasons are changing, it is easy to catch a cold and since colds are transmitted via the respiratory system, wearing a mask on crowded public buses or the MRT can help prevent transmission.

During the winter months, people on scooters wear masks to stay warm and also to filter out air pollution. Servers in restaurants wear masks to keep particles from unintentionally landing in food. Hospital workers and patients wear masks to prevent viral infections. People often wear surgical masks to help stay healthy and help prevent transmission of diseases.

▲ Wearing surgical masks in MRT stations

▲ Wearing surgical masks in the hospital
《聯合報》魯永明 / 攝影

Self-Assessment Checklist

I can ask someone how they are feeling.

20%　　40%　　60%　　80%　　100%

I can describe symptoms in simple terms.

20%　　40%　　60%　　80%　　100%

I can make suggestions to somebody who is sick.

20%　　40%　　60%　　80%　　100%

I can politely accept or reject suggestions.

20%　　40%　　60%　　80%　　100%

Pinyin	Traditional Characters	Simplified Characters	Lesson-Dialogue-Number
A			
a	啊	啊	3-1-21
a	啊	啊	13-1-4
ǎi	矮	矮	10-2-9
B			
ba	吧	吧	3-2-9
ba	吧	吧	10-1-10
bǎ	把	把	15-1-17
bàba	爸爸	爸爸	2-1-20
bǎi	百	百	4-1-15
Bái Rúyù	白如玉	白如玉	3-2-1
bàn	半	半	7-2-6
bāng	幫	帮	4-1-13
bàngqiú	棒球	棒球	3-1-7
bāo	包	包	15-2-16
bǎoxiǎn	保險	保险	15-2-10
bāozi	包子	包子	4-1-8
bēi	杯	杯	4-1-6
bǐ	比	比	8-2-8
biànlì shāngdiàn	便利商店	便利商店	8-1-20
bié	別	别	15-2-14
bǐjiào	比較	比较	8-1-8
bīng	冰	冰	15-2-13
bǐsài	比賽	比赛	7-2-7
bíshuǐ	鼻水	鼻水	15-1-4
bómǔ	伯母	伯母	2-2-2
bù	不	不	1-2-11
bù hǎo	不好	不好	5-2-17
bù xíng	不行	不行	8-2-12
búbì kèqì	不必客氣	不必客气	13-1-22
búcuò	不錯	不错	5-2-12
búguò	不過	不过	11-2-12
bùhǎo yìsi	不好意思	不好意思	11-2-15
búkèqì	不客氣	不客气	1-1-22

Pinyin	Traditional Characters	Simplified Characters	Lesson-Dialogue-Number
búyòng le	不用了	不用了	15-2-20
C			
cài	菜	菜	3-2-16
cānguān	參觀	参观	8-2-2
cāntīng	餐廳	餐厅	5-2-2
chá	茶	茶	1-2-3
chā	差	差	15-1-8
chābùduō	差不多	差不多	8-2-14
cháguǎn	茶館	茶馆	9-2-12
cháng	常	常	3-1-10
chànggē	唱歌	唱歌	7-1-3
chāoshì	超市	超市	11-1-8
Chén Yuèměi	陳月美	陈月美	1-1-1
chéngjī	成績	成绩	12-1-11
chēpiào	車票	车票	8-1-10
chī	吃	吃	3-2-14
chīchīkàn	吃吃看	吃吃看	10-1-15
chīfàn	吃飯	吃饭	6-2-10
chòu dòufǔ	臭豆腐	臭豆腐	5-1-20
chuān	穿	穿	10-2-4
chuānghù	窗戶	窗户	10-2-13
chuántǒng	傳統	传统	13-2-9
chúfáng	廚房	厨房	11-1-4
chūntiān	春天	春天	14-1-5
chūqù	出去	出去	9-1-8
cì	次	次	15-2-6
cóng	從	从	7-1-6
D			
dà	大	大	4-1-10
dǎ	打	打	3-1-5
dà bùfèn	大部分	大部分	13-2-15
dǎ diànhuà	打電話	打电话	11-1-23
Dà'ān	大安	大安	7-1-12
dàgài	大概	大概	9-1-9

Pinyin	Traditional Characters	Simplified Characters	Lesson-Dialogue-Number
dài	帶	带	9-2-4
dàjiā	大家	大家	14-2-10
dàlóu	大樓	大楼	6-2-14
dàn	蛋	蛋	13-2-7
dàngāo	蛋糕	蛋糕	13-2-11
dāngrán	當然	当然	13-1-8
dànshì	但是	但是	8-1-12
dào	到	到	5-2-15
dào	到	到	11-1-12
dào	到	到	12-1-17
dǎsuàn	打算	打算	9-1-3
dàxué	大學	大学	12-1-7
de	的	的	2-1-3
de	得	得	5-2-9
děi	得	得	7-1-8
děng	等	等	11-2-9
děng yíxià	等一下	等一下	7-2-20
diàn	店	店	5-1-14
diǎn	點	点	5-1-16
diǎn	點	点	7-1-1
diànhuà	電話	电话	11-1-20
diànshì	電視	电视	9-1-4
diànyǐng	電影	电影	3-2-5
dìdi	弟弟	弟弟	10-2-11
dìfāng	地方	地方	6-1-15
dìng	訂	订	13-2-3
dòng	棟	栋	6-2-13
dōngtiān	冬天	冬天	14-1-10
dōngxi	東西	东西	6-2-6
dōu	都	都	2-1-13
duì	對	对	10-1-11
duì	對	对	13-2-12
duìbùqǐ	對不起	对不起	1-2-18
duìle	對了	对了	7-1-15
duō	多	多	2-1-11
duō jiǔ	多久	多久	9-1-13
duōshǎo	多少	多少	4-1-2
dùzi	肚子	肚子	15-2-3

Pinyin	Traditional Characters	Simplified Characters	Lesson-Dialogue-Number
F			
fāngbiàn	方便	方便	6-2-2
fángdōng	房東	房东	11-1-2
fàngjià	放假	放假	9-1-10
fángjiān	房間	房间	11-1-15
fángzi	房子	房子	2-1-7
fángzū	房租	房租	11-2-2
fāshāo	發燒	发烧	15-1-12
fāyán	發炎	发炎	15-1-10
fēicháng	非常	非常	8-1-11
fēn	分	分	7-1-4
fēng	風	风	14-1-3
fēngjǐng	風景	风景	6-1-8
fēnzhōng	分鐘	分钟	11-1-10
fù	付	付	11-2-13
fùjìn	附近	附近	6-1-17
fùmǔ	父母	父母	14-1-9
G			
gāng	剛	刚	7-2-3
gānjìng	乾淨	干净	10-2-12
gǎnmào	感冒	感冒	15-1-13
gāo	高	高	10-2-10
gāotiě	高鐵	高铁	8-1-18
ge	個	个	2-2-10
gēge	哥哥	哥哥	2-2-6
gěi	給	给	10-1-4
gěi	給	给	11-1-21
gēn	跟	跟	8-1-3
gēn	跟	跟	15-2-11
gèng	更	更	14-2-9
gōnggòng qìchē	公共汽車（公車）	公共汽车（公车）	8-2-11
gōngkè	功課	功课	9-1-7
gōngsī	公司	公司	12-1-13
gōngzuò	工作	工作	12-2-1
gōngzuò	工作	工作	12-2-8
guàng	逛	逛	9-2-10

Pinyin	Traditional Characters	Simplified Characters	Lesson-Dialogue-Number
guānxīn	關心	关心	15-2-15
gǔdài	古代	古代	8-2-3
Gùgōng Bówùyuàn	故宮博物院（故宮）	故宫博物院（故宫）	8-2-9
guì	貴	贵	4-2-11
guò	過	过	13-1-15
guójiā	國家	国家	12-2-10

H

Pinyin	Traditional Characters	Simplified Characters	Lesson-Dialogue-Number
hái	還	还	9-2-6
hǎi	海	海	6-1-11
háishì	還是	还是	3-2-8
hàn	和	和	3-1-8
hào	號	号	9-2-3
hǎo	好	好	1-1-14
hǎo	好	好	2-1-9
hǎo	好	好	12-2-6
hǎo a	好啊	好啊	3-1-23
hǎo bù hǎo	好不好	好不好	3-2-18
hǎochī	好吃	好吃	5-1-4
hǎode	好的	好的	4-1-17
hǎohē	好喝	好喝	1-2-5
hǎojiǔ bújiàn	好久不見	好久不见	13-1-21
hǎokàn	好看	好看	2-1-16
hǎowán	好玩	好玩	3-1-16
hǎoxiàng	好像	好像	11-2-7
hē	喝	喝	1-2-2
hěn	很	很	1-2-4
hóngsè	紅色	红色	10-1-8
hóngyè	紅葉	红叶	14-1-13
hóulóng	喉嚨	喉咙	15-1-9
hòumiàn	後面	后面	6-1-12
hòutiān	後天	后天	7-1-11
huā	花	花	12-1-9
Huālián	花蓮	花莲	6-1-22
huángsè	黃色	黄色	10-1-2
huānyíng	歡迎	欢迎	1-1-19
huáxuě	滑雪	滑雪	14-1-4
huì	會	会	5-2-10

Pinyin	Traditional Characters	Simplified Characters	Lesson-Dialogue-Number
huì	會	会	11-2-8
huí jiā	回家	回家	15-2-22
huíguó	回國	回国	9-1-2
huílái	回來	回来	13-1-3
huíqù	回去	回去	11-1-17
huǒchē	火車	火车	8-1-2
huòshì	或是	或是	8-1-16

J

Pinyin	Traditional Characters	Simplified Characters	Lesson-Dialogue-Number
jǐ	幾	几	2-2-9
jǐ	幾	几	15-2-5
jiā	家	家	2-1-5
jiā	家	家	5-1-13
jiān	間	间	11-1-13
jiǎngxuéjīn	獎學金	奖学金	12-1-10
jiànkāng	健康	健康	15-2-9
jiànkāng zhōngxīn	健康中心	健康中心	15-2-21
jiànmiàn	見面	见面	7-1-5
jiànyì	建議	建议	9-2-7
jiào	叫	叫	1-1-16
jiāo	教	教	5-2-14
jiāohuàn	交換	交换	13-1-10
jiàoshì	教室	教室	6-2-17
jiārén	家人	家人	2-1-4
jiāyóu	加油	加油	12-1-22
jīchē	機車	机车	8-2-5
jìchéngchē	計程車	计程车	8-2-13
jìde	記得	记得	13-1-7
jiē	接	接	1-1-9
jiějie	姐姐	姐姐	2-1-18
jiěmèi	姐妹	姐妹	2-2-13
jiéshù	結束	结束	7-2-8
jiéyùn	捷運	捷运	8-2-7
jìhuà	計畫	计画	12-1-1
jīhuì	機會	机会	10-1-13
jìn	近	近	6-2-1
jīnnián	今年	今年	13-2-2
jīntiān	今天	今天	3-2-2

Pinyin	Traditional Characters	Simplified Characters	Lesson-Dialogue-Number
jiù	舊	旧	4-2-5
jiù	就	就	9-2-15
jiù	就	就	11-1-11
jiǔ	久	久	12-1-3
juéde	覺得	觉得	3-1-15
juédìng	決定	决定	9-2-13

K

Pinyin	Traditional Characters	Simplified Characters	Lesson-Dialogue-Number
kāfēi	咖啡	咖啡	1-2-14
kāishǐ	開始	开始	7-2-15
kāixīn	開心	开心	10-2-3
kàn	看	看	3-2-4
kànbìng	看病	看病	15-2-8
kànshū	看書	看书	2-2-8
kè	課	课	7-2-14
kěpà	可怕	可怕	14-2-12
kěshì	可是	可是	5-2-3
kètīng	客廳	客厅	11-1-3
kěyǐ	可以	可以	3-2-10
kěyǐ	可以	可以	5-2-13
kěyǐ	可以	可以	7-2-18
kōng	空	空	11-1-14
kuài	塊	块	4-1-16
kuài	塊	快	10-1-5
kuài	快	块	8-1-9
kuài	快	快	14-1-8
kuàilè	快樂	快乐	13-1-2
KTV	KTV	KTV	7-1-2

L

Pinyin	Traditional Characters	Simplified Characters	Lesson-Dialogue-Number
là	辣	辣	5-2-4
lái	來	来	1-1-5
lánqiú	籃球	篮球	3-1-11
lánsè	藍色	蓝色	10-2-15
lǎobǎn	老闆	老板	4-1-4
lǎoshī	老師	老师	2-2-7
le	了	了	4-2-6
le	了	了	13-2-4
lèi	累	累	12-1-20
lěng	冷	冷	14-1-2

Pinyin	Traditional Characters	Simplified Characters	Lesson-Dialogue-Number
Lǐ Mínghuá	李明華	李明华	1-1-2
liǎng	兩	两	2-2-15
liǎnsè	臉色	脸色	15-2-1
lǐmiàn	裡面	里面	6-2-8
Lín	林	林	11-1-22
liú	流	流	15-1-3
lǐwù	禮物	礼物	13-2-1
lóu	樓	楼	6-2-12
lóuxià	樓下	楼下	6-1-18
lǚguǎn	旅館	旅馆	10-2-6
lǚxíng	旅行	旅行	9-1-6

M

Pinyin	Traditional Characters	Simplified Characters	Lesson-Dialogue-Number
ma	嗎	吗	1-1-8
Mǎ Āntóng	馬安同	马安同	2-1-2
mài	賣	卖	4-2-12
mǎi	買	买	4-1-5
māma	媽媽	妈妈	2-1-21
màn	慢	慢	8-1-6
màn zǒu	慢走	慢走	14-2-17
máng	忙	忙	7-2-10
mángguǒ	芒果	芒果	10-1-3
Māokōng	貓空	猫空	9-2-16
méi	沒	没	2-2-11
měi	美	美	6-1-9
měi	每	每	7-2-11
méi guānxi	沒關係	没关系	11-2-16
méi wèntí	沒問題	没问题	7-1-14
Měiguó	美國	美国	1-2-17
mèimei	妹妹	妹妹	2-1-19
ménkǒu	門口	门口	13-1-17
miàn	麵	面	5-1-2
miànxiàn	麵線	面线	13-2-6
míngnián	明年	明年	14-1-11
míngtiān	明天	明天	3-1-17
míngzi	名字	名字	2-2-4

N

Pinyin	Traditional Characters	Simplified Characters	Lesson-Dialogue-Number
ná	拿	拿	15-1-16
nà	那	那	11-2-10

Pinyin	Traditional Characters	Simplified Characters	Lesson-Dialogue-Number
nà / nèi	那	那	4-2-10
nǎ / něi	哪	哪	1-2-12
nǎ guó / něi guó	哪國	哪国	1-2-19
nàlǐ	那裡	那里	6-1-7
nǎlǐ	哪裡	哪里	6-1-5
Nǎlǐ, nǎlǐ	哪裡，哪裡	哪里，哪里	13-2-14
nàme	那麼	那么	12-2-13
nàme	那麼	那么	13-1-11
nán	男	男	10-2-8
nán	難	难	12-2-12
nánkàn	難看	难看	15-2-2
ne	呢	呢	1-2-9
nèiyòng	內用	內用	4-1-19
néng	能	能	4-2-8
nǐ	你	你	1-1-4
nǐ	妳	妳	3-2-6
nǐ hǎo	你好	你好	1-1-23
nián	年	年	12-1-2
niàn	念	念	12-1-6
niánqīng	年輕	年轻	13-2-10
niànshū	念書	念书	12-1-19
nǐmen	你們	你们	1-1-17
nín	您	您	2-2-3
niúròu	牛肉	牛肉	5-1-1
Niǔyuē	紐約	纽约	14-1-16
nǚ	女	女	9-2-1

P

Pinyin	Traditional Characters	Simplified Characters	Lesson-Dialogue-Number
pà	怕	怕	5-2-5
pāi	拍	拍	10-2-1
pángbiān	旁邊	旁边	6-2-16
péi	陪	陪	15-2-7
péngyǒu	朋友	朋友	6-1-20
piányí	便宜	便宜	4-2-13
piàoliàng	漂亮	漂亮	2-1-6

Q

Pinyin	Traditional Characters	Simplified Characters	Lesson-Dialogue-Number
qí	騎	骑	8-2-4
qián	錢	钱	4-1-3
qiān	千	千	4-2-16

Pinyin	Traditional Characters	Simplified Characters	Lesson-Dialogue-Number
qiánmiàn	前面	前面	6-1-10
qǐng	請	请	1-2-1
qǐng	請	请	10-1-14
qǐng jìn	請進	请进	2-1-22
qǐngwèn	請問	请问	1-1-20
qiūtiān	秋天	秋天	14-1-12
qù	去	去	3-1-19
qùnián	去年	去年	12-2-2

R

Pinyin	Traditional Characters	Simplified Characters	Lesson-Dialogue-Number
rè	熱	热	4-1-7
rén	人	人	1-2-7
rèshuǐqì	熱水器	热水器	11-2-6
rèxīn	熱心	热心	13-1-12
Rìběn	日本	日本	1-2-16

S

Pinyin	Traditional Characters	Simplified Characters	Lesson-Dialogue-Number
sǎn	傘	伞	14-2-2
shān	山	山	6-1-13
shàng cì	上次	上次	14-2-16
shàng ge yuè	上個月	上个月	10-2-18
shàngbān	上班	上班	12-1-18
shāngdiàn	商店	商店	6-2-9
shàngkè	上課	上课	6-1-21
shàngwǎng	上網	上网	4-2-9
shānshàng	山上	山上	6-1-4
shǎo	少	少	5-1-6
shéi	誰	谁	2-1-17
shēngbìng	生病	生病	15-1-11
shēngrì	生日	生日	13-1-1
shēngrì kuàilè	生日快樂	生日快乐	13-1-19
shēngyì	生意	生意	12-2-4
shénme	什麼	什么	1-2-6
shì	是	是	1-1-6
shì	試	试	12-2-11
shī	濕	湿	14-2-6
shì a	是啊	是啊	5-1-18
shí'èryuè dǐ	十二月底	十二月底	14-1-18
shìde	是的	是的	1-1-21
shíhòu	時候	时候	7-1-10

Pinyin	Traditional Characters	Simplified Characters	Lesson-Dialogue-Number
shíjiān	時間	时间	12-1-4
shìshìkàn	試試看	试试看	12-2-15
shōudào	收到	收到	11-2-14
shǒujī	手機	手机	4-2-3
shū	書	书	2-2-5
shūfǎ	書法	书法	7-2-13
shūfú	舒服	舒服	8-1-14
shuì	睡	睡	15-2-17
shuǐ	水	水	15-1-18
shuǐguǒ	水果	水果	10-1-1
shuìjiào	睡覺	睡觉	15-1-20
shuō	說	说	5-1-5
suǒyǐ	所以	所以	5-2-6
sùshè	宿舍	宿舍	6-2-11

T

Pinyin	Traditional Characters	Simplified Characters	Lesson-Dialogue-Number
tā	他	他	1-2-10
tā	她	她	9-2-5
tài	太	太	4-2-4
tài hǎo le	太好了	太好了	5-1-21
tài kèqì	太客氣	太客气	13-1-23
Táidōng	臺東	台东	9-1-14
táifēng	颱風	台风	14-2-3
Táinán	臺南	台南	8-1-17
tàitai	太太	太太	10-2-7
Táiwān	臺灣（＝台灣）	台湾（＝台湾）	1-1-18
tāmen	他們	他们	6-1-1
tāng	湯	汤	5-1-10
tàofáng	套房	套房	11-1-16
tǎoyàn	討厭	讨厌	14-2-7
tèbié	特別	特别	9-2-11
tì	替	替	12-1-14
tī	踢	踢	3-1-13
tián	甜	甜	10-1-7
tiān	天	天	7-2-12
tiándiǎn	甜點	甜点	5-2-11
tiānqì	天氣	天气	14-1-1
Tiánzhōng Chéngyī	田中誠一	田中诚一	2-2-1

Pinyin	Traditional Characters	Simplified Characters	Lesson-Dialogue-Number
tíng	停	停	14-2-13
tīng	聽	听	3-1-2
tīngshuō	聽說	听说	6-1-23
tòng	痛	痛	15-1-6
tóngxué	同學	同学	8-2-1
tóu	頭	头	15-1-5
tù	吐	吐	15-2-4
túshūguǎn	圖書館	图书馆	6-2-15

W

Pinyin	Traditional Characters	Simplified Characters	Lesson-Dialogue-Number
wàidài	外帶	外带	4-1-18
wàimiàn	外面	外面	6-2-7
wán	玩	玩	8-1-4
wàn	萬	万	4-2-15
wǎn	碗	碗	5-1-17
wǎnfàn	晚飯	晚饭	3-2-15
wǎng	往	往	10-2-14
Wáng Kāiwén	王開文	王开文	1-1-3
wàngle	忘（了）	忘（了）	13-1-6
wǎnglù shàng	網路上	网路上	8-1-19
wǎngqiú	網球	网球	3-1-6
wǎnshàng	晚上	晚上	3-2-3
wànshì rúyì	萬事如意	万事如意	13-2-16
wéi	喂	喂	11-2-1
wéibō	微波	微波	4-1-14
wèikǒu	胃口	胃口	15-1-7
wèishénme	為什麼	为什么	4-2-17
wèn	問	问	7-2-19
wèntí	問題	问题	11-2-5
wǒ	我	我	1-1-11
wǒ jiù shì	我就是	我就是	13-1-20
wǒmen	我們	我们	1-1-10
wǔ	五	五	2-2-14
wǔcān	午餐	午餐	7-2-2
Wūlóng chá	烏龍茶	乌龙茶	1-2-15

X

Pinyin	Traditional Characters	Simplified Characters	Lesson-Dialogue-Number
xià cì	下次	下次	7-1-13
xià ge xīngqí	下個星期	下个星期	9-1-11
xiàkè	下課	下课	7-2-4

Pinyin	Traditional Characters	Simplified Characters	Lesson-Dialogue-Number
xiān	先	先	12-1-5
xiǎng	想	想	3-2-7
xiǎng	想	想	11-1-18
xiǎng	想	想	14-1-6
xiāng	香	香	10-1-6
xiānshēng	先生	先生	1-1-13
xiànzài	現在	现在	6-1-16
xiào	笑	笑	10-2-2
xiǎo	小	小	4-1-12
xiǎochī	小吃	小吃	5-1-8
xiǎojiě	小姐	小姐	1-1-7
xiǎolóngbāo	小籠包	小笼包	5-1-19
xiǎoshí	小時	小时	15-2-18
xiǎoxīn	小心	小心	14-2-11
xiàtiān	夏天	夏天	14-2-5
xiàwǔ	下午	下午	7-2-5
xiàxuě	下雪	下雪	14-1-17
xiàyǔ	下雨	下雨	14-2-14
Xībānyá	西班牙	西班牙	13-1-18
Xībānyá wén	西班牙文	西班牙文	13-1-13
xiě	寫	写	7-2-17
xièxie	謝謝	谢谢	1-1-22
xīguā	西瓜	西瓜	10-1-9
xíguàn	習慣	习惯	11-2-4
xǐhuān	喜歡	喜欢	1-2-8
xīn	新	新	4-2-2
xìng	姓	姓	1-1-15
xīngqí	星期	星期	9-1-1
xīnnián	新年	新年	14-1-7
xīnwén	新聞	新闻	14-2-8
xīnxiǎng shìchéng	心想事成	心想事成	13-2-17
xiōngdì	兄弟	兄弟	2-2-12
xiūxí	休息	休息	15-1-19
xīwàng	希望	希望	12-1-15
xué	學	学	3-2-11
xuéfèi	學費	学费	12-1-12
xuéshēng	學生	学生	6-2-4

Pinyin	Traditional Characters	Simplified Characters	Lesson-Dialogue-Number
xuéxiào	學校	学校	6-1-2
xūyào	需要	需要	12-1-8

Y

Pinyin	Traditional Characters	Simplified Characters	Lesson-Dialogue-Number
yào	要	要	1-2-13
yào	要	要	4-1-9
yào	要	要	4-2-14
yào	要	要	14-2-4
yào	藥	药	15-1-14
yàojú	藥局	药局	15-1-15
yàoshì	要是	要是	9-2-14
yě	也	也	3-1-12
yèshì	夜市	夜市	9-2-8
yìdiǎn	一點	一点	13-2-8
yídìng	一定	一定	5-1-15
yīfú	衣服	衣服	10-2-5
yígòng	一共	一共	4-1-1
yǐhòu	以後	以后	12-1-16
yǐhòu	以後	以后	12-2-5
yǐjīng	已經	已经	11-2-3
yīnggāi	應該	应该	9-2-9
yǐngpiàn	影片	影片	9-1-5
yínháng	銀行	银行	7-1-9
yīnwèi	因為	因为	10-2-16
yīnyuè	音樂	音乐	3-1-3
yìqǐ	一起	一起	3-2-13
yǐqián	以前	以前	10-1-12
yīshēng	醫生	医生	15-1-1
yíyàng	一樣	一样	13-1-14
yìzhí	一直	一直	15-1-2
yóu	油	油	15-2-12
yòu	又	又	8-1-13
yǒu	有	有	2-1-10
yǒu kòng	有空	有空	7-1-16
yǒu shì	有事	有事	7-2-21
yǒu shíhòu	有時候	有时候	9-1-12
yǒu yìdiǎn	有一點	有一点	5-2-16
yǒu yìsi	有意思	有意思	7-2-22

Pinyin	Traditional Characters	Simplified Characters	Lesson-Dialogue-Number
yòubiān	右邊	右边	11-1-6
yǒumíng	有名	有名	5-1-7
yǒuxiàn diànshì	有線電視	有线电视	11-2-17
yóuyǒng	游泳	游泳	3-1-9
yóuyǒngchí	游泳池	游泳池	6-2-18
yǔ	雨	雨	14-2-1
yuǎn	遠	远	6-1-6
yuè	月	月	9-2-2
Yuènán	越南	越南	3-2-17
yùndòng	運動	运动	3-1-4
Yùshān	玉山	玉山	14-1-15
yùshì	浴室	浴室	11-1-7
yǔyán	語言	语言	13-1-9
yǔyán zhōngxīn	語言中心	语言中心	12-1-21

Z

Pinyin	Traditional Characters	Simplified Characters	Lesson-Dialogue-Number
zài	在	在	6-1-3
zài	在	在	6-2-5
zài	在	在	7-2-1
zài	載	载	8-2-6
zài	再	再	11-1-19
zài	再	再	12-2-14
zàijiàn	再見	再见	7-1-17
zǎo yìdiǎn	早一點	早一点	15-1-21
zǎoshàng	早上	早上	3-1-18
zěnme	怎麼	怎么	8-1-5
zěnme	怎麼	怎么	13-1-5
zěnme le	怎麼了	怎么了	15-2-19
zěnmeyàng	怎麼樣	怎么样	3-1-20
zhàn	站	站	8-1-15
zhāng	張	张	2-1-15
Zhāng Yíjūn	張怡君	张怡君	2-1-1
zhǎo	找	找	6-1-19
zhǎo	找	找	12-2-7
zhàopiàn	照片	照片	2-1-12
zhàoxiàng	照相	照相	2-1-14
zhè / zhèi	這	这	1-1-12
zhè cì	這次	这次	14-2-15
zhèlǐ	這裡	这里	6-2-3
zhème	這麼	这么	5-1-11

Pinyin	Traditional Characters	Simplified Characters	Lesson-Dialogue-Number
zhēn	真	真	5-1-3
zhēnde	真的	真的	6-1-14
zhèxiē	這些	这些	10-2-19
zhèyàng	這樣	这样	12-2-9
zhǐ	只	只	14-1-14
zhī	支	支	4-2-1
zhīdào	知道	知道	5-1-12
zhǒng	種	种	4-2-7
zhōng	中	中	4-1-11
Zhōngguó	中國	中国	8-2-10
zhōngtóu	鐘頭	钟头	8-1-7
Zhōngwén	中文	中文	3-2-12
zhōngwǔ	中午	中午	7-1-7
zhōumò	週末	周末	3-1-1
zhù	住	住	10-2-17
zhù	祝	祝	13-2-13
zhuāng	裝	装	11-2-11
zhūjiǎo	豬腳	猪脚	13-2-5
zì	字	字	7-2-16
zìjǐ	自己	自己	5-2-7
zǒulù	走路	走路	11-1-9
zū	租	租	11-1-1
zuì	最	最	5-1-9
zuìhǎo	最好	最好	15-2-23
zuìjìn	最近	最近	7-2-9
zuò	坐	坐	2-1-8
zuò	坐	坐	8-1-1
zuò	做	做	12-2-3
zuò shénme	做什麼	做什么	3-1-22
zuǒbiān	左邊	左边	11-1-5
zuòfàn	做飯	做饭	5-2-8
zuótiān	昨天	昨天	5-2-1
zuǒyòu	左右	左右	13-1-16
zúqiú	足球	足球	3-1-14

English definition	Traditional Characters	Simplified Characters	Lesson-Dialogue-Number
A			
a bit earlier	早一點	早一点	15-1-21
(a) few	幾	几	15-2-5
a little	有一點	有一点	5-2-16
a little, some	一點	一点	13-2-8
about the same	差不多	差不多	8-2-14
to access the internet, to use the internet	上網	上网	4-2-9
afternoon	下午	下午	7-2-5
afterwards	以後	以后	12-2-5
again	再	再	12-2-14
all, both	都	都	2-1-13
already	已經	已经	11-2-3
also	也	也	3-1-12
altogether	一共	一共	4-1-1
America	美國	美国	1-2-17
ancient times	古代	古代	8-2-3
and, as well as	和	和	3-1-8
annoying	討厭	讨厌	14-2-7
appetite	胃口	胃口	15-1-7
approximately	左右	左右	13-1-16
approximately, about, probably	大概	大概	9-1-9
arrive	到	到	11-1-12
to ask	問	问	7-2-19
at	在	在	6-2-5
aunt; here a polite term for a friend's mother regardless of age	伯母	伯母	2-2-2
autumn (season)	秋天	秋天	14-1-12
B			
back	後面	后面	6-1-12
bank	銀行	银行	7-1-9
baseball	棒球	棒球	3-1-7
basketball	籃球	篮球	3-1-11

English definition	Traditional Characters	Simplified Characters	Lesson-Dialogue-Number
bathroom	浴室	浴室	11-1-7
to be	是	是	1-1-6
to be able to, can	會	会	5-2-10
beautiful	美	美	6-1-9
because	因為	因为	10-2-16
beef	牛肉	牛肉	5-1-1
before	以前	以前	10-1-12
to begin, to start	開始	开始	7-2-15
birthday	生日	生日	13-1-1
blue	藍色	蓝色	10-2-15
book	書	书	2-2-5
both...and...	又	又	8-1-13
a bowl of	碗	碗	5-1-17
boy-, male-	男	男	10-2-8
brothers	兄弟	兄弟	2-2-12
bus	公共汽車 （公車）	公共汽车 （公车）	8-2-11
business	生意	生意	12-2-4
busy	忙	忙	7-2-10
to be busy, to be engaged	有事	有事	7-2-21
but, however	可是	可是	5-2-3
but, however	但是	但是	8-1-12
to buy	買	买	4-1-5
by the way	對了	对了	7-1-15
Bye. Take care.	慢走	慢走	14-2-17
C			
cable TV	有線電視	有线电视	11-2-17
cake	蛋糕	蛋糕	13-2-11
to be called, i.e., to have the first name xx	叫	叫	1-1-16
calligraphy	書法	书法	7-2-13
can, to be able to	能	能	4-2-8
to be careful, to take care	小心	小心	14-2-11
to catch/have a cold	感冒	感冒	15-1-13

English definition	Traditional Characters	Simplified Characters	Lesson-Dialogue-Number
to celebrate	過	过	13-1-15
cell phone	手機	手机	4-2-3
certainly, of course	當然	当然	13-1-8
character	字	字	7-2-16
cheap, inexpensive	便宜	便宜	4-2-13
China	中國	中国	8-2-10
Chinese language	中文	中文	3-2-12
Chinese last name, common in Taiwan	林	林	11-1-22
class	課	课	7-2-14
classmate	同學	同学	8-2-1
classroom	教室	教室	6-2-17
clean	乾淨	干净	10-2-12
clothes	衣服	衣服	10-2-5
coffee	咖啡	咖啡	1-2-14
cold	風	风	14-1-2
to come	來	来	1-1-5
to come back	回來	回来	13-1-3
comfortable	舒服	舒服	8-1-14
company	公司	公司	12-1-13
complement marker	得	得	5-2-9
to be concerned about	關心	关心	15-2-15
continuously, all the way	一直	一直	15-1-2
convenience store	便利商店	便利商店	8-1-20
convenient	方便	方便	6-2-2
to cook	做飯	做饭	5-2-8
correct, right	對	对	10-1-11
could (possibility)	可以	可以	3-2-10
could (possibility)	可以	可以	5-2-13
country	國家	国家	12-2-10
cuisine	菜	菜	3-2-16
cup	杯	杯	4-1-6

D

English definition	Traditional Characters	Simplified Characters	Lesson-Dialogue-Number
Da-an (name of a KTV named after a district in Taipei, where Shida is also located)	大安	大安	7-1-12
dad	爸爸	爸爸	2-1-20

English definition	Traditional Characters	Simplified Characters	Lesson-Dialogue-Number
date, day of a month	號	号	9-2-3
to decide	決定	决定	9-2-13
delicious	好吃	好吃	5-1-4
dessert	甜點	甜点	5-2-11
dinner	晚飯	晚饭	3-2-15
disposal marker	把	把	15-1-17
do what	做什麼	做什么	3-1-22
to do, to engage in	做	做	12-2-3
doctor	醫生	医生	15-1-1
Don't mention it. It's my pleasure.	哪裡，哪裡	哪里，哪里	13-2-14
don't (used in imperatives)	別	别	15-2-14
dormitory	宿舍	宿舍	6-2-11
downstairs	樓下	楼下	6-1-18
to drink	喝	喝	1-2-2

E

English definition	Traditional Characters	Simplified Characters	Lesson-Dialogue-Number
easy to	好	好	12-2-6
to eat	吃	吃	3-2-14
egg	蛋	蛋	13-2-7
the end of December	十二月底	十二月底	14-1-18
with enthusiasm	熱心	热心	13-1-12
even (more, less, etc.)	更	更	14-2-9
evening, night	晚上	晚上	3-2-3
every, each	每	每	7-2-11
everyone	大家	大家	14-2-10
Excellent. Great.	太好了	太好了	5-1-21
to exchange	交換	交换	13-1-10
to exercise	運動	运动	3-1-4
expensive	貴	贵	4-2-11
extra fine noodles	麵線	面线	13-2-6

F

English definition	Traditional Characters	Simplified Characters	Lesson-Dialogue-Number
to fall ill	生病	生病	15-1-11
family (members)	家人	家人	2-1-4
far	遠	远	6-1-6
fast	快	快	8-1-9
to feel, to think	覺得	觉得	3-1-15
few in number	少	少	5-1-6
film	影片	影片	9-1-5

English definition	Traditional Characters	Simplified Characters	Lesson-Dialogue-Number
fine, well	好	好	1-1-14
to finish	結束	结束	7-2-8
to finish class	下課	下课	7-2-4
first	先	先	12-1-5
five	五	五	2-2-14
to flow	流	流	15-1-3
for	幫	帮	4-1-13
for here	內用	内用	4-1-19
for, on behalf of	替	替	12-1-14
to forget	忘（了）	忘（了）	13-1-6
fragrant	香	香	10-1-6
friend	朋友	朋友	6-1-20
from	從	从	7-1-6
front	前面	前面	6-1-10
fruit	水果	水果	10-1-1
in the future	以後	以后	12-1-16

G

English definition	Traditional Characters	Simplified Characters	Lesson-Dialogue-Number
game, competition	比賽	比赛	7-2-7
gate, entrance	門口	门口	13-1-17
general measure word	個	个	2-2-10
to get	拿	拿	15-1-16
to get settled down, to get used to	習慣	习惯	11-2-4
gift, present	禮物	礼物	13-2-1
girl-, female-	女	女	9-2-1
to give	給	给	10-1-4
to give someone a ride to someone on / in a vehicle e.g. bicycle or car	載	载	8-2-6
to give it a try, to try and see what happens	試試看	试试看	12-2-15
to go	去	去	3-1-19
to go back, to return	回去	回去	11-1-17
go home	回家	回家	15-2-22
to go out	出去	出去	9-1-8
to go to class	上課	上课	6-1-21
to go to work	上班	上班	12-1-18
to go/come to	到	到	12-1-17

English definition	Traditional Characters	Simplified Characters	Lesson-Dialogue-Number
to go/stay with somebody, to accompany	陪	陪	15-2-7
Goodbye.	再見	再见	7-1-17
good-looking	好看	好看	2-1-16
grades	成績	成绩	12-1-11

H

English definition	Traditional Characters	Simplified Characters	Lesson-Dialogue-Number
half	半	半	7-2-6
happy	開心	开心	10-2-3
happy	快樂	快乐	13-1-2
Happy Birthday.	生日快樂	生日快乐	13-1-19
hard to, difficult to	難	难	12-2-12
to have	有	有	2-1-10
to have a fever	發燒	发烧	15-1-12
to have a holiday	放假	放假	9-1-10
to have a meal	吃飯	吃饭	6-2-10
to have a taste, try it, taste it	吃吃看	吃吃看	10-1-15
to have free time	有空	有空	7-1-16
to have fun	玩	玩	8-1-4
to have to, must	得	得	7-1-8
he, him	他	他	1-2-10
head	頭	头	15-1-5
health	健康	健康	15-2-9
health center	健康中心	健康中心	15-2-21
hear that	聽說	听说	6-1-23
here, this place	這裡	这里	6-2-3
High Speed Rail (HSR)	高鐵	高铁	8-1-18
home, house	家	家	2-1-5
homework	功課	功课	9-1-7
to hope	希望	希望	12-1-15
hot	熱	热	4-1-7
hot (spicy)	辣	辣	5-2-4
hotel	旅館	旅馆	10-2-6
hour	鐘頭	钟头	8-1-7
hour	小時	小时	15-2-18
house	房子	房子	2-1-7
how	怎麼	怎么	8-1-5

English definition	Traditional Characters	Simplified Characters	Lesson-Dialogue-Number
How about it? How does that sound? What do you think?	怎麼樣	怎么样	3-1-20
How about...? How does that sound?	好不好	好不好	3-2-18
How are you? Hello.	你好	你好	1-1-23
How come?	怎麼	怎么	13-1-5
how long	多久	多久	9-1-13
how many	幾	几	2-2-9
how much, how many	多少	多少	4-1-2
however, but	不過	不过	11-2-12
Hualien, name of a city on the eastern coast of Taiwan	花蓮	花莲	6-1-22
hundred	百	百	4-1-15

I

English definition	Traditional Characters	Simplified Characters	Lesson-Dialogue-Number
I, me	我	我	1-1-11
I'm sorry.	對不起	对不起	1-2-18
icy	冰	冰	15-2-13
if	要是	要是	9-2-14
to be inflamed	發炎	发炎	15-1-10
inside	裡面	里面	6-2-8
to install	裝	装	11-2-11
insurance	保險	保险	15-2-10
interesting, fun	好玩	好玩	3-1-16
to be interesting, to be fun	有意思	有意思	7-2-22
on the Internet	網路上	网络上	8-1-19
It would be best.../ (You) should…	最好	最好	15-2-23
It's not necessary.	不用了	不用了	15-2-20

J

English definition	Traditional Characters	Simplified Characters	Lesson-Dialogue-Number
Japan	日本	日本	1-2-16
job, work	工作	工作	12-2-8
just now	剛	刚	7-2-3

K

English definition	Traditional Characters	Simplified Characters	Lesson-Dialogue-Number
Karaoke	KTV	KTV	7-1-2
keep up the good work	加油	加油	12-1-22
to kick	踢	踢	3-1-13

English definition	Traditional Characters	Simplified Characters	Lesson-Dialogue-Number
kind, type	種	种	4-2-7
kitchen	廚房	厨房	11-1-4
to know	知道	知道	5-1-12

L

English definition	Traditional Characters	Simplified Characters	Lesson-Dialogue-Number
landlord	房東	房东	11-1-2
language	語言	语言	13-1-9
language center	語言中心	语言中心	12-1-21
large	大	大	4-1-10
last month	上個月	上个月	10-2-18
last time	上次	上次	14-2-16
last year	去年	去年	12-2-2
later	等一下	等一下	7-2-20
to laugh, to smile	笑	笑	10-2-2
to learn, to study	學	学	3-2-11
left (side)	左邊	左边	11-1-5
library	圖書館	图书馆	6-2-15
light repast, snack	小吃	小吃	5-1-8
to like	喜歡	喜欢	1-2-8
to listen	聽	听	3-1-2
living room	客廳	客厅	11-1-3
to be located at	在	在	6-1-3
long (time)	久	久	12-1-3
long time no see	好久不見	好久不见	13-1-21
to look for	找	找	12-2-7
lunch	午餐	午餐	7-2-2

M

English definition	Traditional Characters	Simplified Characters	Lesson-Dialogue-Number
to make a phone call	打電話	打电话	11-1-23
a man from Japan	田中誠一	田中诚一	2-2-1
a man from Taiwan	李明華	李明华	1-1-2
a man from the Republic of Honduras	馬安同	马安同	2-1-2
a man from the US	王開文	王开文	1-1-3
mango	芒果	芒果	10-1-3
many	多	多	2-1-11
Maokong, name of a must-see place in Taipei to visit for fine tea and scenery	貓空	猫空	9-2-16
Mass Rapid Transit (MRT)	捷運	捷运	8-2-7

English definition	Traditional Characters	Simplified Characters	Lesson-Dialogue-Number
may (permission)	可以	可以	7-2-18
May all your wishes come true.	心想事成	心想事成	13-2-17
May everything go your way.	萬事如意	万事如意	13-2-16
May I ask you..., Excuse me,…	請問	请问	1-1-20
measure word for bags, packages etc.	包	包	15-2-16
measure word for cell phones	支	支	4-2-1
measure word for Chinese money	塊	块	4-1-16
measure word for day	天	天	7-2-12
measure word for flat objects (e.g., paper, tickets)	張	张	2-1-15
measure word for houses, rooms, etc.	間	间	11-1-13
measure word for minutes	分鐘	分钟	11-1-10
measure word for pieces of food (e.g., meat, cake)	塊	块	10-1-5
measure word for times, occurrences	次	次	15-2-6
measure word for year	年	年	12-1-2
measure word for buildings	棟	栋	6-2-13
measure word for restaurants, shops, etc.	家	家	5-1-13
medicine	藥	药	15-1-14
medium	中	中	4-1-11
to meet	見面	见面	7-1-5
to meet, to see	找	找	6-1-19
to microwave	微波	微波	4-1-14
minute	分	分	7-1-4
to miss (someone)	想	想	14-1-6
Miss, Ms.	小姐	小姐	1-1-7
modification marker	的	的	2-1-3
mom	媽媽	妈妈	2-1-21
money	錢	钱	4-1-3

English definition	Traditional Characters	Simplified Characters	Lesson-Dialogue-Number
month of a year	月	月	9-2-2
(comparatively) more	比較	比较	8-1-8
morning	早上	早上	3-1-18
most	最	最	5-1-9
most (of), mostly	大部分	大部分	13-2-15
motorcycle, scooter	機車	机车	8-2-5
mountain	山	山	6-1-13
on a mountain, in the mountains	山上	山上	6-1-4
movie	電影	电影	3-2-5
Mr.	先生	先生	1-1-13
a multi-storey building	大樓	大楼	6-2-14
music	音樂	音乐	3-1-3

N

English definition	Traditional Characters	Simplified Characters	Lesson-Dialogue-Number
name	名字	名字	2-2-4
National Palace Museum	故宮博物院（故宮）	故宫博物院（故宫）	8-2-9
near	近	近	6-2-1
to need	需要	需要	12-1-8
new	新	新	4-2-2
New Year	新年	新年	14-1-7
New York	紐約	纽约	14-1-16
news	新聞	新闻	14-2-8
next time	下次	下次	7-1-13
next week	下個星期	下个星期	9-1-11
next year	明年	明年	14-1-11
night market	夜市	夜市	9-2-8
No need to stand on formalities, i.e., It's my pleasure.	不必客氣	不必客气	13-1-22
No problem.	沒問題	没问题	7-1-14
noodles	麵	面	5-1-2
noon	中午	中午	7-1-7
not	不	不	1-2-11
not	沒	没	2-2-11
Not a problem.	沒關係	没关系	11-2-16
not bad	不錯	不错	5-2-12
(here) to not like, to fear	怕	怕	5-2-5

English definition	Traditional Characters	Simplified Characters	Lesson-Dialogue-Number
not to look good	難看	难看	15-2-2
not well	不好	不好	5-2-17
now	現在	现在	6-1-16

O

English definition	Traditional Characters	Simplified Characters	Lesson-Dialogue-Number
O.K.	好啊	好啊	3-1-23
O.K.	好的	好的	4-1-17
O.K.	好	好	2-1-9
ocean	海	海	6-1-11
o'clock	點	点	7-1-1
often	常	常	3-1-10
oily, greasy	油	油	15-2-12
old	舊	旧	4-2-5
older brother	哥哥	哥哥	2-2-6
older sister	姐姐	姐姐	2-1-18
only, merely	就	就	11-1-11
only, merely	只	只	14-1-14
Oolong tea	烏龍茶	乌龙茶	1-2-15
opportunity	機會	机会	10-1-13
or	或是	或是	8-1-16
or (used in a question)	還是	还是	3-2-8
to order (meals)	點	点	5-1-16
to order (something in advance)	訂	订	13-2-3
outside	外面	外面	6-2-7

P

English definition	Traditional Characters	Simplified Characters	Lesson-Dialogue-Number
painful	痛	痛	15-1-6
parents	父母	父母	14-1-9
a particle indicating a realization	啊	啊	13-1-4
a particle used in addressing people, especially over the phone	喂	喂	11-2-1
to pay	付	付	11-2-13
person, people	人	人	1-2-7
a person's "color" (said of the face when healthy or sick, pleased or angry etc.)	臉色	脸色	15-2-1
pharmacy, drug store	藥局	药局	15-1-15
photo	照片	照片	2-1-12

English definition	Traditional Characters	Simplified Characters	Lesson-Dialogue-Number
to pick sb up	接	接	1-1-9
place	地方	地方	6-1-15
to plan to	打算	打算	9-1-3
to plan to	計畫	计划	12-1-1
to play (ball games)	打	打	3-1-5
please	請	请	1-2-1
Please come in!	請進	请进	2-1-22
poor, bad	差	差	15-1-8
pork knuckles	豬腳	猪脚	13-2-5
pretty	漂亮	漂亮	2-1-6
problem, question	問題	问题	11-2-5
progressive aspect verb; in the process of doing something	在	在	7-2-1

R

English definition	Traditional Characters	Simplified Characters	Lesson-Dialogue-Number
rain	雨	雨	14-2-1
to rain	下雨	下雨	14-2-14
to read	看書	看书	2-2-8
really	真	真	5-1-3
really must, definitely	一定	一定	5-1-15
really, truly	真的	真的	6-1-14
to receive	收到	收到	11-2-14
recently, lately	最近	最近	7-2-9
red	紅色	红色	10-1-8
red maple leaves	紅葉	红叶	14-1-13
to remember	記得	记得	13-1-7
to rent	租	租	11-1-1
rent (for a room or a house)	房租	房租	11-2-2
restaurant	餐廳	餐厅	5-2-2
to return to one's country	回國	回国	9-1-2
to ride	騎	骑	8-2-4
right (side)	右邊	右边	11-1-6
room	房間	房间	11-1-15

S

English definition	Traditional Characters	Simplified Characters	Lesson-Dialogue-Number
say	說	说	5-1-5
scary	可怕	可怕	14-2-12
scenery, landscape	風景	风景	6-1-8
scholarship	獎學金	奖学金	12-1-10

English definition	Traditional Characters	Simplified Characters	Lesson-Dialogue-Number
school	學校	学校	6-1-2
to see a doctor	看病	看病	15-2-8
to see, to watch	看	看	3-2-4
to seem to be, to appear to be (often used to take the edge off of a comment)	好像	好像	11-2-7
self	自己	自己	5-2-7
to sell	賣	卖	4-2-12
sentence final particle	嗎	吗	1-1-8
sentence final particle	呢	呢	1-2-9
sentence-final particle	啊	啊	3-1-21
sentence-final particle for guessing	吧	吧	10-1-10
sentence-final particle for suggestion	吧	吧	3-2-9
sentence-final particle indicating the speaker's sense of certainty	了	了	4-2-6
she, her	她	她	9-2-5
shop, store	店	店	5-1-14
short (height)	矮	矮	10-2-9
should	應該	应该	9-2-9
(by the) side, next to	旁邊	旁边	6-2-16
to sing	唱歌	唱歌	7-1-3
sisters	姐妹	姐妹	2-2-13
to sit	坐	坐	2-1-8
to ski	滑雪	滑雪	14-1-4
to sleep	睡覺	睡觉	15-1-20
to sleep	睡	睡	15-2-17
slow	慢	慢	8-1-6
small	小	小	4-1-12
snot, nasal mucus, a running nose	鼻水	鼻水	15-1-4
to snow	下雪	下雪	14-1-17
so	這麼	这么	5-1-11
so (very)	那麼	那么	13-1-11
soccer	足球	足球	3-1-14
sometimes	有時候	有时候	9-1-12
soon	快	快	14-1-8
sorry	不好意思	不好意思	11-2-15

English definition	Traditional Characters	Simplified Characters	Lesson-Dialogue-Number
soup, broth	湯	汤	5-1-10
Spain	西班牙	西班牙	13-1-18
the Spanish language	西班牙文	西班牙文	13-1-13
special	特別	特别	9-2-11
to spend (time or money)	花	花	12-1-9
spring (season)	春天	春天	14-1-5
station	站	站	8-1-15
to stay	住	住	10-2-17
steamed buns with meat stuffing filling	包子	包子	4-1-8
still, additionally	還	还	9-2-6
stinky tofu (fermented tofu)	臭豆腐	臭豆腐	5-1-20
stomach, abdomen	肚子	肚子	15-2-3
to stop	停	停	14-2-13
store, shop	商店	商店	6-2-9
store-owner, boss	老闆	老板	4-1-4
a storey, a floor	樓	楼	6-2-12
student	學生	学生	6-2-4
to study	念	念	12-1-6
to study	念書	念书	12-1-19
suggestion	建議	建议	9-2-7
suite, studio	套房	套房	11-1-16
summer (season)	夏天	夏天	14-2-5
supermarket	超市	超市	11-1-8
to be surnamed	姓	姓	1-1-15
sweet (taste)	甜	甜	10-1-7
to swim	游泳	游泳	3-1-9
swimming pool	游泳池	游泳池	6-2-18

T

English definition	Traditional Characters	Simplified Characters	Lesson-Dialogue-Number
Taiwan	臺灣（＝台灣）	台湾（＝台湾）	1-1-18
Tainan, a city in southwestern Taiwan	臺南	台南	8-1-17
Taitung, name of one of the major cities on the south eastern coast of Taiwan	臺東	台东	9-1-14
to take	帶	带	9-2-4
to take (pictures)	拍	拍	10-2-1

English definition	Traditional Characters	Simplified Characters	Lesson-Dialogue-Number
to take a photo	照相	照相	2-1-14
to take a rest	休息	休息	15-1-19
to take by, to travel by	坐	坐	8-1-1
take out, to go	外帶	外带	4-1-18
to take, to require	要	要	4-2-14
tall	高	高	10-2-10
(lit. good to drink) to taste good	好喝	好喝	1-2-5
taxi	計程車	出租车	8-2-13
tea	茶	茶	1-2-3
to teach	教	教	5-2-14
teacher	老師	老师	2-2-7
teahouse	茶館	茶馆	9-2-12
telephone	電話	电话	11-1-20
ten thousand	萬	万	4-2-15
tennis	網球	网球	3-1-6
(more...) than	比	比	8-2-8
thank you	謝謝	谢谢	1-1-22
that	那	那	4-2-10
that place, there	那裡	那里	6-1-7
That's right.	是啊	是啊	5-1-18
That's very kind of you.	太客氣	太客气	13-1-23
the day after tomorrow	後天	后天	7-1-11
the same, alike	一樣	一样	13-1-14
then	就	就	9-2-15
and then	再	再	11-1-19
then	那麼	那么	12-2-13
then, in that case	那	那	11-2-10
therefore, so	所以	所以	5-2-6
these	這些	这些	10-2-19
they (used for people only)	他們	他们	6-1-1
things, stuff	東西	东西	6-2-6
to think	想	想	11-1-18
this	這	这	1-1-12
(said of self on the phone) This is s/he speaking.	我就是	我就是	13-1-20
this kind (of)	這樣	这样	12-2-9

English definition	Traditional Characters	Simplified Characters	Lesson-Dialogue-Number
this time	這次	这次	14-2-15
this year	今年	今年	13-2-2
thousand	千	千	4-2-16
throat	喉嚨	喉咙	15-1-9
to throw up, to vomit	吐	吐	15-2-4
(train, bus) ticket	車票	车票	8-1-10
time	時間	时间	12-1-4
tired	累	累	12-1-20
to	到	到	5-2-15
to	給	给	11-1-21
to	對	对	13-2-12
to	跟	跟	15-2-11
today	今天	今天	3-2-2
together	一起	一起	3-2-13
tomorrow	明天	明天	3-1-17
too	太	太	4-2-4
toward, to	往	往	10-2-14
tradition, customs	傳統	传统	13-2-9
train	火車	火车	8-1-2
to travel	旅行	旅行	9-1-6
to treat sb to sth	請	请	10-1-14
to try	試	试	12-2-11
tuition	學費	学费	12-1-12
TV	電視	电视	9-1-4
two	兩	两	2-2-15
typhoon	颱風	台风	14-2-3

U

English definition	Traditional Characters	Simplified Characters	Lesson-Dialogue-Number
umbrella	傘	伞	14-2-2
university	大學	大学	12-1-7

V

English definition	Traditional Characters	Simplified Characters	Lesson-Dialogue-Number
vacant, empty	空	空	11-1-14
verbal particle indicating a completed action	了	了	13-2-4
very	很	很	1-2-4
very	非常	非常	8-1-11
vicinity, near	附近	附近	6-1-17
Vietnam	越南	越南	3-2-17
to visit (an institution)	參觀	参观	8-2-2

English definition	Traditional Characters	Simplified Characters	Lesson-Dialogue-Number
W			
to wait for	等	等	11-2-9
to walk	走路	走路	11-1-9
to wander around, to look around	逛	逛	9-2-10
to want to	要	要	1-2-13
to want, to need	要	要	4-1-9
to want, to think	想	想	3-2-7
water	水	水	15-1-18
water heater	熱水器	热水器	11-2-6
watermelon	西瓜	西瓜	10-1-9
we, us	我們	我们	1-1-10
to wear, to put on	穿	穿	10-2-4
weather	天氣	天气	14-1-1
week	星期	星期	9-1-1
weekend	週末	周末	3-1-1
welcome	歡迎	欢迎	1-1-19
well known, famous	有名	有名	5-1-7
wet	濕	湿	14-2-6
what	什麼	什么	1-2-6
What's wrong?	怎麼了	怎么了	15-2-19
when	時候	时候	7-1-10
where	哪裡	哪里	6-1-5
which	哪	哪	1-2-12
Which country?	哪國	哪国	1-2-19
who	誰	谁	2-1-17
why	為什麼	为什么	4-2-17
wife	太太	太太	10-2-7
will	會	会	11-2-8
will not do	不行	不行	8-2-12
will, be going to	要	要	14-2-4
wind	冷	冷	14-1-3
window	窗戶	窗户	10-2-13
winter (season)	冬天	冬天	14-1-10
to wish (somebody happiness, good luck, etc.)	祝	祝	13-2-13
with	跟	跟	8-1-3
a woman from Taiwan	張怡君	张怡君	2-1-1

English definition	Traditional Characters	Simplified Characters	Lesson-Dialogue-Number
a woman from the US	白如玉	白如玉	3-2-1
a woman from Vietnam	陳月美	陈月美	1-1-1
to work	工作	工作	12-2-1
to write	寫	写	7-2-17
X			
xiaolongbao, e.g., small meat and cabbagefilled steamed buns	小籠包	小笼包	5-1-19
Y			
yellow	黃色	黄色	10-1-2
yes	是的	是的	1-1-21
yesterday	昨天	昨天	5-2-1
you	你	你	1-1-4
you (female)	妳	妳	3-2-6
you (honorific)	您	您	2-2-3
you (plural)	你們	你们	1-1-17
You're welcome.	不客氣	不客气	1-1-22
young	年輕	年轻	13-2-10
younger brother	弟弟	弟弟	10-2-11
younger sister	妹妹	妹妹	2-1-19
Yu Shan (Mount Jade), tallest mountain in central Taiwan	玉山	玉山	14-1-15

第十一课　我要租房子

对话一

如　玉：林先生，你好，我是白如玉，来看房子。
房　东：白小姐，妳好，请进。
房　东：这里是客厅，厨房在左边，右边有浴室。
如　玉：房子很不错。
房　东：这里很方便，附近有超市和捷运站，走路五分钟就到了。
如　玉：现在有人住吗？
房　东：有。还有两间空房间，一间是套房，一间不是。
如　玉：我想看套房。房间里面可以上网吗？
房　东：可以。妳觉得这间房间怎么样？妳想租吗？
如　玉：我回去想想，再打电话给你。

对话二

如　玉：喂，房东先生，你好，我是白如玉，你收到我的房租了吗？
房　东：我已经收到了，谢谢。妳习惯了吗？
如　玉：习惯了。可是，有一个问题，热水器的水好像不热。
房　东：今天我会去看看。妳什么时候有空？晚上可以吗？
如　玉：不好意思，今天晚上我有事。
房　东：没关系，明天下午呢？
如　玉：好，我在家等你。
房　东：那我明天下午两点到。还有问题吗？
如　玉：我想买电视。请问可以帮我装有线电视吗？
房　东：可以，不过妳得自己付钱。
如　玉：好的，谢谢你。

第十二课　你计画在台湾学多久的中文？

对话一

田　中：安同，你计画在台湾学多久的中文？
安　同：五年。
田　中：为什么要这么久的时间？
安　同：我先在语言中心念一年，再念四年大学，所以需要五年。
田　中：这得花不少钱！
安　同：对，不过我有奖学金。要是成绩不好，就没奖学金了。你呢？
田　中：我的学费是公司替我付的。
安　同：你打算学多久呢？
田　中：大概两年，是公司决定的。
安　同：希望我以后也可以到这么好的公司上班。
田　中：我又要上班，又要念书，真的很累。

安　同：我们一起加油吧！

对话二

月　美：田中，你是什么时候来台湾工作的？
田　中：去年，我已经在台湾工作一年了。
月　美：为什么你们公司要替你付学费？
田　中：因为我们公司跟台湾人做生意。老板希望我们都会说中文。
月　美：我觉得你们公司真好。
田　中：对了，妳回国以后，打算做什么？
月　美：我回国以后，也想找个有机会说中文的工作。
田　中：不错，这样的工作在你们国家好找吗？
月　美：不知道好不好找，我试试看。
田　中：要是难找呢？
月　美：那么我再来台湾学中文。
田　中：太好了！那我们就可以再见面了。

第十三课　生日快乐

对话一

怡　君：喂，安同吗？
安　同：是，我就是。怡君，好久不见，听说妳去花莲？
怡　君：我没去花莲，我刚从台东回来。
安　同：找我有什么事？
怡　君：明天是你的生日，对不对？
安　同：啊，我怎么忘了！最近太忙了，谢谢妳还记得。
怡　君：当然记得！语言交换的时候，你那么热心教我西班牙文。
安　同：不必客气，妳也一样。
怡　君：明天我想请你吃晚饭，给你过生日。
安　同：妳太客气了！我们在哪里见面呢？
怡　君：明天我一下课，就去你们学校找你。
安　同：大概几点？
怡　君：五点左右。
安　同：好，我会在学校门口等妳。

对话二

安　同：怡君，谢谢妳请我到这么有名的餐厅吃饭。
怡　君：哪里，哪里！这是我给你的礼物。
安　同：谢谢！真开心，今年有台湾朋友给我过生日。
怡　君：你想吃什么？有没有不吃的东西？
安　同：我什么都吃。
怡　君：我已经订了猪脚面线和蛋。等一下你多吃一点。
安　同：台湾人过生日是不是都吃这些东西？

怡　君：对啊！这是传统，不过，现在大部分年轻人过生日不吃这些东西了。

安　同：那么，你们过生日吃什么呢？

怡　君：跟你们一样，吃蛋糕。今天我也订了一个生日蛋糕。

安　同：妳对我真好。

怡　君：安同，祝你生日快乐、万事如意、心想事成。

安　同：谢谢！谢谢！

第十四课　天气这么冷！

对话一

如　玉：外面风那么大，我觉得今天比昨天冷。台湾会不会下雪？

明　华：很高的山会下雪。玉山常下雪。美国呢？开始下雪了吧？

如　玉：还没有。每年差不多十二月开始。下雪的时候，我常去山上滑雪。

明　华：我怕冷。我比较喜欢春天。

如　玉：春天不错，天气很舒服。

明　华：我去年五月在纽约玩了两个星期。那个时候，天气很好，风景也很漂亮，我玩得非常开心。

如　玉：我在台湾住了半年多了。有一点想家。

明　华：新年快到了。想回去看父母吗？

如　玉：我打算十二月底回去。想跟我去美国玩吗？

明　华：冬天太冷了。不过，我想明年秋天去看红叶。对了，妳什么时候回来？

如　玉：因为我们只放十天的假，所以一月五号回来。

对话二

明　华：如玉，雨下得这么大，妳怎么没带伞呢？

如　玉：我昨天带了，可是今天忘了带。

明　华：台风快要来了。

如　玉：我已经听说了。

明　华：这里每年夏天都有台风。台风来的时候，风和雨都很大，做什么都很不方便。

如　玉：是啊！哪里都湿湿的。真讨厌。

明　华：电视新闻说，这次的台风会比上次的更大，请大家多小心。

如　玉：希望这次的没有上次的那么可怕。

明　华：如玉，妳看！雨停了。

如　玉：太好了！谢谢你的伞，再见。

明　华：不客气。小心慢走。

第十五课　我很不舒服

对话一

医　生：白小姐，妳哪里不舒服？

如　玉：我一直流鼻水，头很痛，胃口很差。什么东西都不想吃。

医　生：大概多久了？

如　玉：已经四、五天了。

医　生：我看看妳的喉咙。喉咙有一点发炎。

如　玉：请问我生的是什么病？

医　生：妳有一点发烧，是感冒，不过没有什么关系。

如　玉：请问我得吃药吗？

医　生：要，妳到药局去拿药。

如　玉：好的。请问我的病什么时候会好？

医　生：回去把药吃了，多喝水，多休息，早一点睡觉，很快就会好。

如　玉：好的，谢谢您。

对话二

如　玉：你怎么了？脸色这么难看。

安　同：昨天晚上肚子很不舒服，吃了东西就吐，还吐了好几次。

如　玉：你这么不舒服，我陪你去看病，好不好？

安　同：不用了。我在台湾没有健康保险。

如　玉：那么，我陪你去学校的健康中心。那里的医生很好，对学生也很客气。

安　同：谢谢妳。我想去药局买药就好了。

如　玉：你真的不去看病吗？

安　同：我想回家休息。请妳跟老师说，我生病了，不能上课。

如　玉：好。你自己要多小心。油的、冰的东西最好都别吃。

安　同：谢谢妳的关心。

（如玉下课以后）

如　玉：我来看你了。现在觉得怎么样？好一点了吗？

安　同：谢谢妳，好多了。我吃了一包药以后，睡得比昨天好。

如　玉：不错。你睡了几个小时的觉以后，现在脸色比早上好得多了。

Linking Chinese

當代中文課程　課本 1-3（二版）

策　劃	國立臺灣師範大學國語教學中心	發 行 人	林載爵
主　編	鄧守信	社　　長	羅國俊
顧　問	Claudia Ross、白建華、陳雅芬	總 經 理	陳芝宇
審　查	姚道中、葉德明、劉 珣	總 編 輯	涂豐恩
編寫教師	王佩卿、陳慶華、黃桂英	副總編輯	陳逸華
英文審查	李 櫻、畢永峨		

執行編輯	張莉萍、張雯雯、張黛琪、蔡如珮	叢書編輯	賴祖兒
英文翻譯	范大龍、張克微、蔣宜臻、龍潔玉	地　　址	新北市汐止區大同路一段 369 號 1 樓
校　對	張莉萍、張雯雯、張黛琪、蔡如珮、	聯絡電話	(02)8692-5588 轉 5305
	李芃、鄭秀娟	郵政劃撥	帳戶第 0100559-3 號
編輯助理	許雅晴、喬愛淳	郵撥電話	(02)23620308
技術支援	李昆璟	印 刷 者	文聯彩色製版印刷有限公司
插　畫	何慎修、張榮傑、黃奕穎	2021 年 10 月初版・2024 年 5 月初版第九刷	
封面設計	Lady Gugu	版權所有・翻印必究	
內文排版	洪伊珊	Printed in Taiwan.	
錄　音	王育偉、王品超、李世揚、吳霈蓁、	ISBN	978-957-08-5971-3 (平裝)
	馬君珮、許伯琴、Michael Tennant	GPN	1011001471
錄音後製	純粹錄音後製公司	定　價	400 元

著作財產權人　國立臺灣師範大學
地址：臺北市和平東路一段 162 號
電話：886-2-7749-5130
網址：http://mtc.ntnu.edu.tw/
E-mail：mtcbook613@gmail.com

感謝

王佩卿、王盈婷、王盈雯、何瑞章、李尚遠、林欣穎、林聖雄、林嫣芳、林蔚儒、徐國欽、張素華、
張瑜庭、莊淑帆、陳宇婕、陳冠引、陳建宏、陳昱蓉、陳韋誠、陳書韋、陳淑美、陳逸達、陳嘉禧、
陳鳳儀、傅聖芳、黃奕穎、楊淩雁、虞永欣、蔡宛蓉、賴瑩玲
協助拍攝本教材及試用教材期間使用之相關照片

udn TV、中央氣象局、《中國顏色》（黃仁達／著、攝）、台北 101、台灣大車隊、
《台灣喫茶》（吳德亮／著、攝）、統一超商、蕙風堂、聯合報
授權提供本教材之相關照片

（以上依姓氏或單位名稱筆畫順序排列）

國家圖書館出版品預行編目資料

當代中文課程 課本1-3（二版）/國立臺灣師範大學國語
教學中心策劃．鄧守信主編．初版．新北市．聯經．
2021年10月．172面．21×28公分（Linking Chiese）
ISBN　978-957-08-5971-3（平裝）
[2024年5月初版第九刷]

1.漢語　2.讀本

802.86　　　　　　　　　　　　　　　　110012624